MW01027757

How to Stay Invisible

MAGGIE C. RUDD

How to Stay Invisible

FARRAR STRAUS GIROUX

NEW YORK

Farrar Straus Giroux Books for Young Readers
An imprint of Macmillan Publishing Group, LLC
120 Broadway, New York, NY 10271 • mackids.com

Our books may be purchased in bulk for promotional, educational, or business use.
Please contact your local bookseller or the Macmillan Corporate and
Premium Sales Department at (800) 221-7945 ext. 5442 or by email at
MacmillanSpecialMarkets@macmillan.com.

Library of Congress Cataloging-in-Publication Data
Names: Rudd, Maggie, author.
Title: How to stay invisible / Maggie C. Rudd.
Description: First edition. | New York : Farrar Straus Giroux Books for Young
Readers, 2023. | Audience: Ages 10–14. | Audience: Grades 4–6. | Summary: When
twelve-year-old Raymond and his pup Rosie are abandoned by his family, he uses his
wilderness skills to survive in the woods, but as winter comes, he realizes his wits are
not enough, and that perhaps it is time he starts trusting others with his secret.
Identifiers: LCCN 2022047023 | ISBN 9780374390334 (hardcover)
Subjects: CYAC: Abandoned children—Fiction. | Survival—Fiction. | Forests and
forestry—Fiction. | Dogs—Fiction. | Trust—Fiction. | Middle schools—Fiction. |
Schools—Fiction.
Classification: LCC PZ7.1.R8279 Ho 2023 | DDC [Fic]—dc23
LC record available at https://lccn.loc.gov/2022047023

First edition, 2023
Book design by Maria Williams
Forest © by ActiveLines/Shutterstock, Leaves © by Lovecta/Shutterstock
Printed in the United States of America by Lakeside Book Company,
Harrisonburg, Virginia

ISBN 978-0-374-39033-4
3 5 7 9 10 8 6 4

For all the kids who have ever felt invisible

How to Stay Invisible

Chapter One

At 4:36 in the afternoon, Raymond Hurley sat waiting in the front office of River Mill Middle School. Apart from the school's basketball team, the only other students in the building were the few who stayed to study in the library. Mrs. Bradsher, the front office secretary, stood with her arms crossed, impatiently tapping the toe of her shoe on the floor, checking her silver wristwatch more often than was necessary. This was not the first occasion that she had been made to stay late waiting on Raymond Hurley. Raymond could hear the little charms on her bracelet impatiently clinking against the watch. The phone rang and Mrs. Bradsher picked it up.

"River Mill Middle—Yes, I'm still here . . . I know I am . . . Yep, same kid . . ." She hung up and crossed her arms again, glaring at Raymond.

Raymond had enrolled in the seventh grade at the middle school only two weeks prior and his mother had been late every day. Some days, he would start walking the three miles home and his mother would pick him up on her way to their trailer, still wearing her clothes from the night before. On other days, Raymond would make it all the way home without passing a single car, tired and sore.

Raymond stood up from the office bench and tried to appear apologetic. "I think I was supposed to walk today," he said. Mrs. Bradsher huffed, rested both hands on her hips, and pinched her lips together.

"Tell that mother of yours that school ends at three thirty," she said. "Some of us have plans."

"Yes ma'am," he said, and hitched his book bag up on his shoulder, pushed the doors open, and began the long walk home. Raymond was used to being forgotten. His mother and father wouldn't win any awards for their parenting, but they were the only family he had so he tried to forgive them. They moved around so much that Raymond never truly unpacked his small collection of belongings. This was his third town and third middle school this year alone and it was only November.

When Raymond was in the fifth grade, his dad got a job roofing houses in a town on the coast and they had stayed put for almost a year. That was the year he found his dog, Rosie, digging through the trash outside a seafood restaurant. He had fallen in love with her instantly, her sandy-brown hair, her stubby legs that were too short for her body, the way she licked his hand instead of smelling him like most dogs would. Raymond remembered one night that year when his mom actually cooked them dinner. Rosie lay at Raymond's feet while they all ate together at their kitchen table. Spaghetti with meatballs and buttered toast. It was the first time they had ever eaten a meal together. That had been the best year of Raymond's life. He kicked a rock along the side of the road.

River Mill was an old farming community, spread out across miles of country highway that paralleled the school. Raymond hadn't spent much time in town. He had only ventured as far as the woods surrounding the small trailer that his parents rented, or he was at school. On a few afternoons, he had gone fishing in the river that ran through the woods between the school and his new home. And on the nights that his parents stayed up late, he would take Rosie to the river and camp out under the stars, thinking about the year that he had lived at the coast, falling asleep to the sounds of the water.

When he finally made it home, it was almost dark. Bright orange and pink rays split the sky as the sun sank into the earth. For a moment, Raymond marveled at how different the sunsets were here in the South. When the sky was clear, you could see every color. Just two months earlier, he had been living in Maryland. And now, somehow, they'd ended up in North Carolina. They were just supposed to be stopping for gas in River Mill but there was a MILL WORKERS WANTED sign posted in the gas station window. Before Raymond knew it, he was being enrolled in school.

Raymond took a deep breath, watching the sunset. He exhaled and adjusted his book bag. His feet and back ached from walking. Rosie was sitting next to a blue duffel bag on the small stoop of their trailer. She jogged forward to meet him and happily licked his outstretched hand. "Hey girl," he said, patting her head. "I missed you too."

Raymond stared down at the duffel bag. It was half-open, sloppily stuffed with his few belongings. He sighed. *We must be moving again*, he thought. He tried the door. It was locked. He cupped his hands to his eyes and peered through the dirty window. "Mom?" he called. "Dad?" Apart from a few pieces of scattered trash in the kitchen, the trailer appeared to be totally deserted.

He went around the side and tried the back door. It was also locked. "Hello?" he called, jostling the doorknob. There was no answer. Raymond looked across the yard. The crickets were beginning to chirp. Feeling nervous, he walked to the front steps and sat down. Rosie, who had followed him around the house, whimpered and leaned in to lick his face.

The light was still on in the rental office across the lot. "Stay," he said to Rosie, and he made his way across the gravel. After a few minutes of knocking, a very hairy, very dirty man answered. He was wearing a stained T-shirt that stretched over his round belly and he was sporting a fat lip full of tobacco. The man scratched his chin, leaned his head out the door, and spat. A brown stream of spit slopped out and trailed back to his chin. "Yeah?" he grunted.

"Er . . . ," said Raymond. "The door is locked to trailer 408. It's getting dark and I can't get in."

"That 408, you say?" The man scratched his belly and adjusted the wad in his lip. "Folks that rented 408 dropped off their keys and left a little after lunch today."

Raymond's brow wrinkled. "Are you sure?"

"Yeah, I'm sure. They left that dog," he said, gesturing to Rosie. "I was just about to call animal control."

Raymond felt like his head was filling with water. He stood frozen, hooked by some invisible line through the throat. He blinked a few times, confused. "She's mine," he said finally.

"I'm just picking her up." Raymond didn't like the way the man was looking at him. He began to back away, hardly noticing that his feet were moving. He tripped over a rock and tried to right himself.

The man looked like he was going to say something else but then he shrugged and said, "If you talk to those folks, tell them they owe me fifty bucks. They never paid no pet deposit for that thing."

Raymond nodded and walked quickly back to Rosie. The man was still watching him from the rental office porch. "Come on, girl," he whispered. Raymond grabbed his things, fumbling with the straps of the bag. "Maybe they went to pick me up from school. Maybe we are taking a trip for Thanksgiving. Maybe I just missed them," he said. That had to be it. He must've been so lost in thought that he hadn't seen their rusty Dodge pass him on the road. Raymond did not allow himself to think anything else. Not yet. His hands were shaking as he grabbed the fishing pole that was propped against the trailer. He gestured for Rosie to follow. He just needed to get back to the school and they would be there waiting for him.

It was a cool night but Raymond had started sweating. He was practically running along the road and his breath was quick and sharp. He unzipped his coat. It was dark now and the road and forest looked different in the light of the moon.

Rosie was walking too close alongside him and he tripped over her. Could she sense his anxiety? "It's okay, girl. We're okay." He tried to sound reassuring but even he didn't buy it.

By the time he made it back to school, he had two bleeding blisters on the backs of his ankles and he was drenched in sweat. The school building was dark but the parking lot was lit up by a single overhead light that automatically turned on when the sun went down. Raymond looked around. There were no cars in the parking lot. His parents weren't waiting for him. His heart sank. His ears were ringing and he shook his head, trying to focus.

He forced himself to take a few deep breaths and decided it was best to get out of the light. Now wasn't the time to panic, he told himself. "Come on, girl," he said to Rosie and walked around the side of the building. He stopped at the spigot in front of the baseball field and drank so much water that his belly bulged. Rosie lapped up the water from the puddle and whined. Raymond made his way to the wooden dugout and dropped the blue duffel bag into the dirt. He set his book bag on the bench and sat down, his fingers gripping the fishing pole.

A car drove by the school and Raymond turned eagerly toward it. He could see the headlights from the baseball field but couldn't make out the model of the car. But it didn't stop. It wasn't them. Rosie licked his hand. "I don't know what happened to them," he said out loud. But he did know. How many times had his parents told him what a burden he was? How often had they said that they would be better off without him? But he never thought that they would actually *leave* him. Sure, his parents had left him at home before for a few nights at a time, sometimes longer. But they had always come back. Raymond had done his best to stay out of trouble and help out as much as he could. He fed himself, took care of whatever house they were living in, and cleaned up after their parties. He had tried. Just last weekend, he'd made plans to make Thanksgiving dinner for them, using all of his meager savings to buy groceries. He'd made Thanksgiving dinner last year too and thought he might make it a tradition. But it didn't matter. They had left him again and this time felt different. This time, they hadn't left him with a place to stay. Where was he supposed to go? How would they know where to find him if they came back? *When* they came back, he corrected himself.

When Raymond was nine, they were living in the mountains and his parents had said they were running out to get dinner. They had been gone for six days when a neighbor reported him living alone. Then the police showed up. He was taken away from the house and placed in a children's home, living with at least twenty other kids. When his parents finally did come back, it took them over a year to get him out of the system. They had promised him that things would be different.

After that, they moved to the coast together. His mom was sober. He found Rosie. Things were better. And then his dad lost his job and his mom stopped trying. Raymond would suffer through anything rather than end up stuck indoors at another children's home, sleeping with one eye open, fighting for his meals, and hiding in bathrooms and broom closets.

Raymond couldn't help but admit that lately his parents

had been getting worse and worse. Forgetting to pick him up, forgetting to get groceries, forgetting to come home. He felt like he should've been more prepared for this.

A canvas sign hung on the baseball fence, shining in the moonlight. SHOP-N-SAVE GROCERY: FROM THE FIELD TO YOUR TABLE. Raymond's stomach growled. Rosie whimpered in agreement. He opened the duffel bag and riffled through the contents. "Aha!" he said, pulling out a pack of peanut butter crackers. He ate the crackers slowly, sharing three with Rosie. He dug through the bag again and pulled out his toothbrush.

In the second grade, a dentist had come to visit Raymond's classroom. He had shown them pictures of teeth with cavities and of mouths rotting from decay. Then he had passed out toothbrushes and toothpaste and little white boxes of dental floss. Ever since that day, Raymond was diligent about his oral hygiene, never forgetting to brush his teeth each morning and night. He walked to the spigot and wet the brush. He hated not having toothpaste but water was better than nothing. He brushed until his gums bled.

Back in the dugout, he leaned his head against the high bench. Rosie turned a few circles and then curled up at his feet. He sat staring past second base and into the night.

Chapter Two

Raymond snapped awake at the sound of car tires on gravel. A burgundy Honda was creeping into the gravel side lot, the first one there. Raymond sat frozen as memories of the day before flooded him. His heart began to thump. He was certain the driver would see him sitting in the dugout. Rosie could feel Raymond's stress. Her ears stood straight up and she nudged his leg, whining. "Shh, Rosie! They'll see us." She whimpered again. "Quiet, girl," he pleaded. He put his hand reassuringly on her neck and she fell silent. "Don't move," Raymond whispered.

His science teacher, Mr. Rosen, got out of the car whistling and walked to the side door. He let himself into the school without a backward glance. As soon as the door clicked shut behind him, Raymond sprang up from the bench. "C'mon, girl!" He grabbed the duffel, his book bag, and his fishing pole and took off in the direction of the woods behind the field.

Raymond paced the tree line as the sun rose. His ears were ringing again. He tried to concentrate but he felt dizzy. Rosie stayed close behind him. He tried to tell her it would be all right but no sound came out. His head was pounding so loudly that he knew someone would hear it. He bent and heaved in the dried leaves, gripping a tree trunk. He slumped to the ground and tried to pull in slow breaths of air. Rosie lay down beside him, pushing her back against his legs. He rubbed her head. "Good girl," he said over and over, finding his voice. "Good girl. Good girl. Good girl."

Raymond took a deep breath. He would just have to look for his parents after school. He could still get a warm breakfast if he went to school and the thought made his stomach clench. He opened his duffel and pulled out a clean shirt. He ran the dry toothbrush over his teeth and tongue and winced at the taste of bile clinging to his throat. That would have to be good enough. He closed up the duffel, set it against a large tree, and piled leaves on top to disguise it. He propped his fishing pole up against another tree close by. "Stay here," he said to Rosie as he lifted his book bag onto his shoulder. "I'll be back after school." She whimpered in protest but lay down by the pile of leaves covering the duffel. Her fur was good camouflage. Raymond turned toward the school.

Getting into the middle school from the woods wasn't as hard as Raymond thought it would be. He walked just inside the tree line, concealing himself until he reached the edge of the woods by the bus lot. He watched as the buses pulled in. Their brakes hissed as they finished for the morning. He waited for kids to pile off and then he slipped into the crowd and into the school cafeteria.

He made himself eat the pancakes slowly, worried that he would vomit again. He took a bite of a sausage patty and then wrapped the rest of it in a napkin, tucking it away for Rosie. He drank all of his milk and peeled an orange, devouring the whole thing.

"Want mine?" a boy asked from the other side of the table. "I don't really like oranges. Or any fruit for that matter. But they always make you get it even if you don't want it." The boy was taller than Raymond by about a foot and Raymond could tell he was too skinny, even sitting down. He had a country accent and his collarbones stood out, prominent from the faded Dale Earnhardt Jr. racing shirt that hung off him, at least two sizes too big. The boy held the orange out to Raymond. "Your name's Raymond, right? You're in my art class." Raymond couldn't remember seeing the boy in art class but then again, he never paid much attention to other kids. He tried to keep his head down at school, blend in. Moving around as much as he did never left much room for making friends and Raymond was out of practice. Raymond reached out and took the orange.

"Thanks," he said.

"I'm Harlin," the boy said. It was quiet for a few seconds and then, "You like cars?"

Raymond shrugged.

"You watch racing?" Harlin asked, taking a bite of his pancake and talking with his mouth full.

"No. Not really," said Raymond.

"I love cars. And pretty much anything to do with racing. One day, I'm gonna fix me up a Chevrolet Camaro and race it at Talladega. That's in Alabama. You ever been to Alabama? Where are you from anyway?" Harlin was one of those people who didn't take breaths between sentences. Or bites.

"We move around a lot."

"That must be cool. I ain't never left River Mill. My dad said he would take me one town over to Commerce for a race but he never did. That's the closest I've ever been to getting anywhere other than here. I live with my gran. She's my dad's mom. I never met my mom's folks."

Raymond nodded. "Thanks again for the orange," he said, getting up.

Harlin swallowed. "Bye then!" he called cheerfully.

Raymond wanted to get away from Harlin and he needed to go to the bathroom before homeroom. He threw the Styrofoam tray in the trash can and slipped past the crowd of students coming in from being dropped off out front. They were hovering around a big *River Mill Winter Jamboree and Bingo Night* poster on the wall in the hallway.

In the bathroom, Raymond splashed water on his face. He sniffed himself. He pulled some brown paper towels from the dispenser and pumped some soap onto them. He unzipped his coat and pulled his T-shirt forward, rubbing the paper towels under his armpits. After he rinsed himself off again, he adjusted his shirt and tried to comb his wiry blond hair with his fingertips. He needed a hairbrush. And some deodorant.

In math, Raymond's first class of the day, the other students were chatting about their plans for the weekend or excitedly talking about the Winter Jamboree. Schoolwork had always come naturally to Raymond and he was usually placed in all the advanced classes. The kids in those classes never paid much attention to him and he preferred it that way. Sure, there was always an initial interest in the new kid but Raymond sat as he always did, avoiding conversation, quietly completing his work without asking questions. Kids usually moved on quickly from being interested in Raymond and River Mill was no different.

"Be ready for a quiz," his math teacher reminded them at the end of class. Mr. Brewer was an ex–football coach and treated his class like a football game. *Drill! Drill! Drill!* The whole class groaned and Mr. Brewer smirked. "Pays to study!" he barked before dismissing them.

The rest of the day seemed to go by very quickly. Raymond moved through each class in a fog, hardly paying attention to Mr. Rosen in science. Nobody asked him any questions and he didn't raise his hand. For lunch, they had sliced turkey and potatoes. He slipped the roll in his pocket with the sausage for Rosie.

In English, Ms. Marcus displayed the question of the day on the board and all the kids got out their notebooks to record their answers. This is how they started each class. The questions were usually simple enough, things like *What do you want to be when you grow up?* Today the question was, *If you could have anything in the world that you wanted, what would it be?* Raymond wrote *Toothpaste.* But then thinking that Ms. Marcus might actually read his entry, he hastily erased it and stared down at the paper. Anything in the world? *Parents,* Raymond thought. But he couldn't write that either. He scribbled down *Spaghetti* and passed his notebook up the row for collection.

Ms. Marcus had a pretty typical classroom. There were quotes from famous authors on the walls and a few posters reminding students to check for grammatical errors. The desks were in neat rows and everything was incredibly clean for a middle school classroom. Ms. Marcus was younger than most of the teachers at River Mill and had a soft demeanor that reminded Raymond of an elementary school teacher he once had. Despite her appearance, she had a reputation for being strict but fair. On the rare occasion that anyone tested her reputation, they quickly learned never to cross her again. Somehow she did this without ever yelling. Raymond liked that about her. And he liked that her classroom was quiet.

Ms. Marcus took up the notebooks and began passing out papers. "Good work, Raymond," she said when she reached his desk. She handed him the vocabulary quiz they had taken the day before. The grade *100* was circled in red at the top of the page. She lowered her voice. "You did better than most, and you weren't even here for half of these words." Raymond tucked the quiz into his bag before anyone else could see it and Ms. Marcus continued down the row.

His last class of the day was art. When Harlin came into the room, he sat down next to Raymond. "Hey buddy!" he said with a grin as he dropped his things, scattering them across the table. "Whoops, sorry 'bout that." He reached across Raymond to retrieve his pencil.

They began working on a collage project, cutting up pictures from magazines. It was supposed to be a self-reflection and Harlin's poster was covered in cars. Raymond felt blank. He thumbed through the magazines but couldn't bring himself to cut out a single picture.

"Raymond?" Raymond looked up. "Can't you hear?" Harlin asked. "I must've called your name like four times."

"Oh sorry," said Raymond.

"I asked if you was gonna cut anything out?"

"Oh. Yeah. Sorry," said Raymond. He grabbed the scissors and absentmindedly started cutting from a magazine page.

"You got a kid brother or something?" asked Harlin.

"What?"

"It's just you're cutting out a Pampers advertisement." Harlin half smiled and raised an eyebrow.

"Oh. Yeah. No," said Raymond, and he balled up the paper.

"You're funny," Harlin said. And then he launched into more car talk, picking up where he'd left off at breakfast. When the bell rang, Raymond put his blank poster back on the pile in the middle of the table. He grabbed his book bag and made his way to the door. "See you tomorrow!" Harlin yelled after him but Raymond didn't turn around. He followed the crowd of students to the bus lot. He checked to make sure nobody was watching and then slipped into the trees.

He found Rosie right where he had left her. He offered her the sausage patty and she gladly accepted, licking his fingers in gratitude. "Come on, girl," he said. He left his things concealed in the woods and headed toward the road. Raymond had never attended a middle school so secluded from the outside world. When it had been built many years before, most of the students came from farms in the area so it was pretty far from town. He was careful to stay hidden in the woods for as long as he could manage and then he stepped out into the sun. The town itself consisted of the Main Street courthouse, a Shop-N-Save grocery store, a Baptist church, and a few run-down shops that sold antiques or odds and ends. He walked along the edge of the road with Rosie trailing behind him, occasionally darting after a squirrel.

When he reached the road that led to town, he turned left in the direction of the sawmill where his father had been working for the past few weeks. When he made it to the mill, cars were pulling out of the parking lot, going home after the workday. The office trailer was still open and he knocked once before he and Rosie walked in.

"No dogs allowed!" the man behind the desk barked.

Raymond jumped. "Sorry," he said quickly, and led Rosie back outside and told her to wait on the porch. She obeyed, looking slightly annoyed. Back in the office, Raymond felt frazzled. On the walk over, he had thought about what he would say when he got there but now that he was here, he didn't know where to start.

"Well?" the man asked, looking at Raymond. "What can I do for you? You're too small to work. Come back when you're older and your parents can sign off."

Raymond would be thirteen in June but he didn't say anything. He was small for his age and had always been on the skinny side. He was used to folks thinking he was younger than he was. Besides, that wasn't why he was here.

"I'm looking for Ray Hurley," he said.

The man made a noise that was a mix between a snort and a laugh. "You ain't the only one," he said. "He didn't show up for work today and he asked for an advance yesterday for the rest of the month's wage." He shook his head. "I shouldn't have given it to him. Should've known better. I'm too softhearted, with the holiday coming up and all. Too trusting. Always have been."

Raymond wondered briefly if the man was related to Harlin. "I'm taking care of his dog and he didn't tell me when he would be back." Raymond had practiced this line on the way there. Bending the truth was something else he had grown used to over the years. With parents like his, it was downright necessary.

"Well, your guess is as good as mine," the man said.

Raymond nodded. "Do you think you could tell him that I'll be at River Mill Middle School? If . . . when he comes back, I mean. He can find me there."

"I doubt he'll be showing his face around here if'n he does come back. But yeah, I'll tell him."

"Thanks," Raymond said, and he left the office. He thought about going to the bus station but he didn't have any money. And besides, where would he go? He had never met any of his grandparents and he didn't have any other family that he knew of. Plus, everything he owned was in the woods behind the school.

The sun was beginning to go down when Raymond retrieved his duffel from behind the school and settled himself against a tree for the rest of the evening. The cold of winter hadn't set in yet but Raymond zipped his coat all the way up anyway. He pulled his math notebook from his book bag and did his homework in the dimming light. He and Rosie shared the leftover roll for dinner and he ate the orange Harlin had given him. He read from a book he had gotten at the school library about a blind boy who was shipwrecked on an island. When he could no longer see the pages, Raymond leaned his head against the tree and fell asleep.

Chapter Three

He woke up freezing. The temperature had dropped in the night. He rubbed his head, shaking the dew from his hair. Rosie was nestled against his hip and he rubbed the wet from her fur as well. He rested his forehead on her small body. "Stay here," he said. "I'll be back after school and we'll figure this out." She licked his ear.

Raymond ate his breakfast in the cafeteria, pocketing some for Rosie. It was the day before Thanksgiving and his stomach was already tight with anticipation of the long weekend ahead.

In homeroom, Raymond checked his cubby in Ms. Marcus's classroom. He pulled out a couple of reminders about grades and requests for supplies, the usual papers that would end up in the trash or scattered around the classroom floors. He found a bright green flyer with information about the annual Winter Jamboree and Bingo Night. Raymond had seen the posters in the halls. There was something else in the back of Raymond's cubby. He reached in and pulled out a brand-new tube of toothpaste. He looked around. Ms. Marcus was sitting at her desk, grading papers. She glanced up briefly and then said, "Jeremy Wallace, you had better pick that paper up off of my floor."

Jeremy gave a little yelp and hurriedly picked up the balled-up paper, threw it in the trash can, and rushed to his seat. Raymond tucked the toothpaste into his book bag. Ms. Marcus signaled for Raymond to come to her desk. "How are you, Raymond? Are you settling in?" Ms. Marcus asked, her tone softening.

"Yes ma'am," he answered.

She set her pen down. "It's hard to be the new kid," she said. Teachers were always saying things like this to Raymond when he started a new school. Most of them didn't really care, but Raymond could tell Ms. Marcus wasn't like most teachers.

He shrugged. "I'm pretty used to it."

"You'll let me know if you need anything?" she asked.

"Yes ma'am," he said again, but he knew he wouldn't. He wouldn't make that mistake again.

She nodded and smiled. "Good." She studied Raymond and it looked like she wanted to say something else but then she picked up the pen and went back to her work. Raymond thought of the toothpaste in his bag. "Thanks," he said, and quickly walked away. He was embarrassed but grateful.

At his last school in Maryland, his math teacher had taken a special interest in Raymond. She noticed how underdressed he was for the weather and had given him his winter coat, something he was very grateful to have. Maryland had been much colder than North Carolina. One day, Mrs. Heineman started asking Raymond if he wanted her to call Social Services for him. Over and over, she asked, every day. Finally, Raymond gave in and said yes. He was just so hungry.

The next week, a lady from Social Services came to Raymond's house. But she didn't even walk up the front porch steps. Instead, she stood awkwardly on the sidewalk, eyes darting from Raymond to her clipboard. Raymond was standing on the porch with his mother, who happened to be home at the time and had come outside at the sound of the car pulling up. The social worker peered around Raymond to the open front door but made no attempt to enter the house.

"Are you okay"—she checked her clipboard again—"Raymond?"

"Yes ma'am," he answered. Then his mother placed her hand on his shoulder and Raymond felt hopeful, like maybe this was the scare that she needed. The children's home had been only two years before, and Raymond thought maybe, just maybe she would remember what it was like to lose him. Maybe she would remember how hard it was to get him back. It had been so long since she had touched him and now she practically had her arm around him.

"We're fine," his mother said in a voice that was too sweet.

Then Raymond and the social worker locked eyes. Raymond could tell right away that she knew. She *knew* everything was not fine. But she looked down at her clipboard when she asked the next question. "Is there anything that you need, Raymond?"

"No ma'am," he said quietly.

"All right then," she said, and made a mark on her paper. "Give me a call if you need anything. Anything at all." She reached forward and handed Raymond a card.

"Thanks, but we're fine," his mother had repeated, her voice already losing its fake pitch. She took the card from Raymond, and the social worker turned to leave. Raymond felt frozen, rooted there by his mother's hand, which was barely touching him now. He watched the social worker walk to her car, climb in, and buckle up. She never looked back. He watched her pull down the street. Then he felt his mother's hand leave his shoulder and she went back into the house.

Raymond stood on the porch for a long time before going inside. His mother was already packing. He wasn't sure what he had wanted to happen. But one thing he *was* sure about was that nobody, not even a social worker, could help him.

Wishing he could run to the bathroom and brush his teeth properly, Raymond walked to the round table in his science class and sat down. On the table was a box of supplies for an experiment. Inside the box were a few packs of chewing gum, scissors, a candle, and a few size-C batteries.

"Using what you know about energy and what you've learned so far about the flow of electrons, I want you to light the candle by the end of class, without using a match or lighter," Mr. Rosen said. A kid threw a paper ball to the front of the room.

Mr. Rosen caught it and threw it back like he was playing a game of basketball.

Raymond looked at the other students sitting at his table. One of the boys had already unwrapped an entire pack of gum and was chewing all of it loudly, folding the gum wrappers into triangle footballs that he flicked to the boy next to him. A red-haired girl sitting next to Raymond peered over the box and said, "Maybe we are supposed to find something to put the batteries in?"

"You can only use the items in the box," Mr. Rosen called to the class, answering. The red-haired girl shrugged. Raymond thought about the batteries. He thought about the gum. How could gum start a fire? One of the gum wrapper footballs flicked him between the eyes and fell to the table. He flinched. Then he picked it up and unwrapped it, scratching the foil with his finger.

Raymond pulled one of the batteries out of the box. He flattened the gum wrapper, then wrapped the battery in the foil, thinking about the flow of electrons. Then he touched the foil side of the wrapper to either end of the battery. Nothing happened. He grabbed the pair of scissors from the box, carefully made the strip of foiled paper thinner, and tried again. He had almost given up when a small stream of smoke drifted up. "Whoa!" the boy said from the other side of the table; the fat wad of gum was stuffed in the side of his cheek.

Raymond smiled, triumphant.

"Can you do that again?" the red-haired girl asked.

"I think so," said Raymond. He took another wrapper and carefully cut a long skinny strip. "Here," he said to the girl, handing her the candle. "Have this ready in case it lights this time."

Raymond repeated the steps and sure enough, smoke drifted up and a tiny flame raced to either end of the paper. The red-haired girl held the candle out just in time and the wick caught fire. The table cheered as Mr. Rosen danced his way over to admire their work.

"Wonderful!" he exclaimed. Mr. Rosen launched into an explanation for the class. "All physical and chemical changes require a source of energy to make them occur. In this case, electrical energy through the flow of electrons in the battery, and thermal energy will drive the process of oxidation, resulting in fire. When you place a thin foil wrapper on each side of the battery, electrons begin to flow from the positive to negative end of the battery because it is conductive (meaning it allows for the flow of electrons and heat)." Mr. Rosen stopped to act out the flow of electrons, waving his arms from side to side.

"The electrons collide with the atoms that make up the foil, and these collisions form thermal or heat energy. Heat will build quickly, and the movement of atoms will increase. As electrons collide and atoms move, they can form new bonds via thermal energy. But that isn't enough." He paused for emphasis. "What else do you need to create a fire?"

Raymond knew the answer immediately but stayed quiet, looking around the room at the glazed-over eyes and the furrowed brows of his classmates.

"Oxygen?" the red-haired girl's uncertain voice whispered.

Mr. Rosen clapped happily. "Oxygen! Yes, Lexi! For a fire to occur, you need oxygen. And oxygen is always looking to make bonds (think carbon dioxide). When oxygen is combined with the thermal energy produced from the wrapper and battery, you get oxidation, and in this case, that means you get fire!" Then Mr. Rosen threw his head back and laughed like an evil scientist, and some students joined in, throwing their heads back and cackling. With Raymond's example and Mr. Rosen's explanation, the students were lighting their candles in no time.

"Nice job, Raymond," the red-haired girl said. Raymond felt his cheeks grow warm. Apart from Harlin, Raymond hadn't thought anyone knew his name.

"Thanks," he said. "You too."

"I'm Lexi." She smiled. "You're new, right?"

Raymond nodded and began putting away the supplies. At the end of class, when he was sure nobody was looking, he grabbed one of the batteries and an unopened pack of gum and slipped them into his pocket.

At lunch, he managed to save half of his ham sandwich and a banana before discarding his lunch trash. He looked into the bins at all the unopened bananas and half-eaten sandwiches. The school cafeteria had a policy that required every student to take one fruit and one vegetable at each meal. Most of which went uneaten and were thrown away at the end of lunch. He thought of Rosie, hungry in the woods. The school custodian, Mr. Ingle, was closing the trash bags. Raymond watched as he wheeled the large bins out of the cafeteria to the dumpsters outside.

Chapter Four

After school, Raymond made his way back to the tree where he had slept the night before. He found the duffel bag easily enough, but Rosie wasn't anywhere in sight. "Rosie!" he called, trying to keep his voice low. "Rosie, come here, girl." He looked around and saw nothing but trees and leaves. He began to panic. "Rosie!" he screamed. Then he saw her. She was standing about fifty feet from him in the woods, wagging her tail. Raymond relaxed.

"Where'd you go?" he asked as she jogged to meet him. He pulled a half-eaten waffle out of his pocket and gave it to her. She ate it in one bite. Then she turned back in the direction she had come, waiting for Raymond to follow. He slung the duffel bag over his shoulder and grabbed the fishing pole.

He followed her into the woods for about a half mile. She was running along in front of him and he had to jog to keep up. Rosie's short legs made it much easier for her to wriggle under the brush while Raymond's pants and coat kept catching on briars. He pulled himself free and asked, "Where are we going, girl?"

When he looked up, Rosie was standing inside of an enormous fallen tree. The roots of the tree had been ripped from the earth and reached out in all directions like a giant sunburst in the woods. The tree's trunk was completely hollowed out.

Raymond stood at the base of the tree and peered inside. Rosie licked his hand, impatient for praise. He leaned in and scratched her ears. "Good girl," he told her.

He walked around the base of the tree, looking for signs of life. Rosie jumped down to follow. Raymond had heard once that fallen trees had been known to spring back upright after a storm. But the root plate of this tree appeared to be totally severed from the earth. Its trunk was sunk into the ground so that it was hard to tell where the tree stopped and the earth began. Raymond didn't think even gale-force winds could budge this monster.

When he was satisfied with its safety, he slung his duffel into the great hollow trunk and crawled in after it. He ducked to avoid hitting his head. The tree didn't falter. Raymond swept out the rot and leaves with his hands, revealing smooth walls. The hollowed inside of the tree was just long enough to lay his fishing pole down in.

He peered outside the tree. This was as good a camp as any, he thought, at least until he could figure something else out. A cold breeze blew in and Raymond pulled his coat tight. He looked out into the quiet woods. He shifted his weight and sat down, leaning against the inside of the trunk. Without realizing it, he began to cry. Silent tears poured from his face and onto his jeans, making a spattered pattern. Rosie jumped in and lay down beside him, resting her head on his leg.

After a few minutes, he pulled himself together. He opened the blue duffel and started removing the contents. Two pairs of jeans, three T-shirts (one dirty, two clean), a few balled-up pairs of socks and underwear, one gray hoodie, a toothbrush, and one small tackle box. He popped the top of the tackle box and thumbed through his small collection of lures. He took out the small fishing knife and then closed the box and packed everything back into the duffel, setting it by his fishing pole.

Another breeze blew in and Raymond shivered. His first task was to stay warm. He needed to build a fire. He and Rosie spent the rest of the afternoon gathering small twigs and sticks. Raymond pulled off loose tree bark and threw it onto the woodpile. They found a small creek not far from the hollowed tree and Rosie drank from its waters. Feeling parched, Raymond cupped his hands to drink from the cool moving waters. He knew he should boil the water before drinking but he needed fire first and something to boil the water in. They followed the small creek to the river and Raymond gathered fist-size rocks to construct a fire ring. When the sun began to set, he and Rosie made their way back to the camp.

Raymond had spent his fair share of time in the woods before now. It was where he often found refuge from his parents on particularly bad nights. Sometimes when he got home from school, if his parents weren't home yet, Raymond would make himself dinner from whatever he could find in the house and then he and Rosie would go to the woods to camp out. It was easier to choose to be alone, rather than have someone force it on you. And being alone was something Raymond was used to.

When Raymond lived at the children's home, kids weren't allowed to leave once they were in for the night. He had longed for the woods and the fresh air. Raymond couldn't even open the window next to his bed while he was there because it had been painted shut. Walking out of that building for the last time had been like coming up for air.

He sat down by the pile of sticks. Raymond had been building fires since elementary school. But he usually had a lighter or a box of matches to help out. Now, he used his fishing knife to strip the fibers from the inside of a piece of tree bark. This he rolled between his fingers, forming a ball that would serve as loose tinder. He knew he would only have a finite amount of time to catch the tiny flame of the gum wrapper and he needed something dry and extra flammable. He cleared an area of ground near the base of his tree shelter and crouched down to work.

He constructed a fire ring with the river rocks. In the middle of the ring, he built a tepee out of twigs and left a small opening. Then he placed the larger sticks around the edges. He pulled the battery and gum pack from his pocket and unwrapped a piece, carefully using his knife to cut the wrapper into four strips. He calculated that he could build twenty fires using the pack of gum. But he was new at this method and it took all four strips and one more from another wrapper to get the flame to ignite the tinder. When it finally did, he stuffed the tinder into the tepee and blew until the twigs caught. Then he sat back to admire his work, feeling rather proud of himself. *I can do this,* he thought.

His stomach growled and he thought of the Thanksgiving groceries and wondered if they were still in the trailer refrigerator. He guessed they would have been cleaned out for the next tenant. What a waste. Last Thanksgiving, they had been living in a tiny studio apartment. Raymond had been couponing for weeks and had purchased two large chicken breasts and fried them in oil. He'd heated green beans from a can and he'd even boiled potatoes and tried to mash them himself. His parents had eaten the meal in silence, taking little bites, like they were nervous or something. His father kept looking at the TV. Then, out of nowhere, his mother slammed her fork on the table.

"What is this?" she asked angrily. "Are you trying to show me what a bad mom I am, huh? I can't even prepare Thanksgiving for you?"

Raymond was shocked. "What? I—" He couldn't answer. He thought they would be happy about the meal.

"I could fix it if I wanted to," she said, and she lifted a spoonful of mashed potatoes and thunked it back into the pan. Then she pushed the chair back and got up. His father mimicked the action, ready to leave. His father was always ready to leave.

Raymond sat at the table while they pulled on coats and boots, muttering and complaining as they left the apartment. He consolidated the food from his parents' plates onto one and set it on the floor for Rosie. She did a little jump before licking it clean. He finished his own dinner and put away the leftovers. He'd made Jell-O too, and he stood at the counter eating straight from the bowl. He washed the dishes, and he and Rosie left the apartment for the woods. Happy Thanksgiving.

Now, Raymond poked the fire with a stick and wondered what it would be like if his parents were here. The thought almost made him laugh out loud. But his smile quickly disappeared and he felt a growing lump in the back of his throat. He swallowed hard, pushing it back down. He stood and shook his head, taking slow shaky breaths.

His parents weren't there. He was alone. Rosie nudged his leg and he bent and rubbed her head. Almost alone.

It was a cold night but the fire would make it bearable. Raymond wondered what he would do when the temperatures really dropped. North Carolina would probably never get as cold as Maryland, but he would need more than just his winter coat and a few twigs and leaves to keep warm.

Raymond shared the half sandwich from his lunch with Rosie and ate the leftover banana. It didn't touch his hunger. His stomach growled in earnest. Trying to ignore it, Raymond grabbed his toothbrush and walked back to the creek to wash up. He cleaned himself up, splashing water on his face. He took a few sips and made a mental note to find some soap.

In the darkness, the shelter of the tree was oddly comforting. Rosie jumped in and Raymond lay down and used the duffel as a pillow. He thought about all the places he had lived and all the schools he had attended. There were too many to count. He thought about the times he had slept in the woods. This felt different somehow.

At the end of elementary school, Raymond's class had gone on a field trip to a wilderness camp. They had spent the day learning how to build a fire, how to set a snare to catch a rabbit, and how to build a trap for small game like mice or squirrels. They even learned which bugs could be eaten in an emergency situation. Raymond shuddered. He hoped he wouldn't need that information.

Raymond shivered and tried to tuck his knees into the bottom of his coat. Somewhere in the woods, a coyote began to howl. Rosie curled up closer and he wrapped an arm around her. He listened nervously to the distant, high-pitched yips and yowls until his eyelids became heavy and he drifted off to sleep.

Chapter Five

On Thanksgiving Day, Raymond spent the early hours of the morning gathering kindling and larger branches to build another fire. He made a pile against the fallen tree. Rosie dragged a few sticks too, helping out.

"That's right, girl. Put them there, right outside the hollow." *The hollow.* He liked the way that sounded.

Rosie chased squirrels up trees and jumped around, making Raymond laugh. "If you can catch one," Raymond called after her, "then we'll really be in business!" His stomach growled.

When he felt good about his stick supply, he grabbed his fishing pole and the small tackle box. He and Rosie followed the creek to the river to see if they could catch some fish.

Raymond picked a spot elevated from the water by a sandbank and large rocks where the river was wide and the sun was shining. There was a man fishing on the opposite bank. Raymond couldn't make out his features but he could see that he was older; his gray hair shone in the sun. The man tipped his hat and Raymond gave a nervous wave.

"There's nothing unusual about fishing in the river on a holiday," Raymond said to himself as he tied on a lure and prepared his rod. After an hour or two of fishing across from the man, Raymond looked up and he was gone.

Raymond caught one small brim and resisted the urge to

take a bite out of it right there at the river. By now, his stomach was writhing with hunger. Feeling pretty pleased with his catch, and unable to wait any longer, he made his way back to camp, fish in tow. He did his best to clean the fish with his knife. He built a fire and skewered the fish to roast. He salivated impatiently as it cooked. Finally, he tore the meat from the fish and ate greedily. "There you go, Rosie girl! Happy Thanksgiving," he said, his mouth full, tossing her a piece. He'd done a poor job preparing the fish, and he pulled small bones from his mouth with every bite. He would definitely need practice filleting fish. Rosie didn't seem to mind, though. After dinner, his stomach still growling, he brushed his teeth, relishing the crisp clean taste of toothpaste. He stretched out in the hollow. He tried not to think of his parents or wonder what their Thanksgiving had looked like without him.

It was a restless night, filled with rustling leaves and unknown noises. Raymond stuffed his hoodie over his head, trying not to listen. His stomach was growling and he couldn't relax enough to fall asleep. When he finally did fall asleep, it was short-lived. Hunger woke him and he gave in, pulling himself from the hollow in the early-morning hours.

He and Rosie fished again at the same spot on the river. After he cast his line, Raymond looked around. He had the odd and distinct feeling that he was being watched, but there was no sign of the man from the day before. He fished for hours without a single bite and decided to walk upriver to try his luck in a different spot.

His stomach churned and Rosie whined. The brim from the night before was long gone. He found a clear spot and sat down on the edge of the river to cast his line. He was too hungry and tired to stand. By midafternoon, Raymond felt the familiar lump in the back of his throat. He blinked against the sun, trying not to cry. *I can do this,* he thought.

Rosie barked, and Raymond looked over. She was pawing at something caught under an embankment. Raymond saw a familiar silver shine. He pulled in his line and went to Rosie. He lay on his stomach and reached his arms under the embankment, pulling out a dead bass. He inspected the fish. It was large but didn't appear to be bloated. It still felt firm, not mushy. He couldn't see any puncture wounds or bite marks. He smelled it. It smelled like fish but not in a bad way.

"What do you think?" he asked Rosie. "Should we risk it?" His stomach groaned in response.

He carried the fish back to the hollow and cleaned it as quickly as possible. It had been almost twenty-four hours since he had last eaten and he was fighting the fatigue of his muscles. He built a fire and roasted the fish. When he could wait no longer, he pulled the fish from the flames and ate greedily. He offered the fish to Rosie but she didn't eat. Raymond shrugged and ate his fill. He brushed his teeth by the fire, too tired to walk to the stream. He zipped up his coat, crawled into the hollow, and fell asleep.

A few hours later, Raymond woke up in a sweat, feeling too hot for the cold night. He was shivering and his stomach was gripped with pain. He immediately thought of the dead bass and pinched his eyes closed again. He should've known better. He *had* known better but he'd eaten it anyway. And now he was going to pay for his mistake.

He pulled himself out of the hollow and removed his coat, letting it fall to the ground. The cold air rushed across his sweat-coated chest and in an instant he felt better and then immediately worse. He doubled over in pain, clutching his stomach. He ran alongside the hollow, leaned against its great trunk, and was sick in the leaves. He slumped to the ground and curled up. He stayed there in the leaves, emptying the contents of his stomach for what seemed like hours. His body shivered and convulsed against the cold, but Raymond couldn't bring himself to get off the ground and find his coat again.

At some point in the night, Rosie was there, licking his forehead. Raymond managed to crawl back to the hollow, finding his coat along the way. But as soon as he was in the tree, he had to pull himself back out for the next wave of sickness. This lasted well into the night and by Saturday morning, he could barely move.

He lay on the ground, stomach completely empty, body completely depleted, staring up into the dappled light of the trees above. He felt a wave of nausea, closed his eyes, and begged for sleep.

When he woke up again, he knew the sickness was over. He could feel the difference in his body. He was weak but no longer ill. He sat up, leaning against the weight of his arms, and swallowed hard. His mouth and throat were dry. He walked to the creek and took small sips of the cool running water. He submerged his hands and washed them off, scooping the cold water onto his face and letting it run down his neck.

He propped himself up against a tree by the water. It had taken every ounce of energy he had left to get him here and he would have to recover to move again. He fell asleep against the tree trunk.

When his eyes opened again, it was almost dusk. His stomach felt like a clenched fist, unable to relax, spasming against emptiness. All he could think of was his hunger. Yet his body protested at the thought of eating. What could he eat? Bark? Leaves? Then, thinking of the dumpster full of discarded food, he made up his mind to walk back to the school.

He moved slowly, and it took him close to an hour to get there. He had to stop to prop himself against a tree every few feet. Rosie walked patiently beside him, staying close. Finally, Raymond watched the school from the tree line. It was late now on a Saturday evening and the school was deserted. Raymond waited nervously. When he felt confident that nobody was around, he crept to the dumpster and peered inside. It was full and smelled terrible. Raymond heaved, but nothing came out. He took a few deep breaths and pulled a trash bag from the top of the pile. He riffled through its contents, trying to breathe through his mouth.

He managed to drag five very ripe bananas, a half-eaten jar of peanut butter, two uneaten apples, and an unopened can of

Vienna sausages back to the shadowy comfort of the woods. He sat in the leaves and slowly ate a banana. At first it was difficult, but each bite gave him new strength. He made his way back to camp, straining to see in the moonlight. He and Rosie sat in the hollow and had a small, quiet feast. With a belly still recovering but much more relaxed, Raymond fell asleep.

Chapter Six

"Good morning, Raymond!" Ms. Marcus said. She was standing by the cafeteria breakfast line as Raymond served himself toast and eggs. "How was your Thanksgiving?"

"It was all right," he responded, trying not to make eye contact. He had spent the entire day on Sunday letting his body recover from illness, and he still didn't feel totally back to normal. "I wasn't feeling well," he said absentmindedly. He was trying to decide if he should get a carton of milk or a bottle of water. His brain told him he needed the calories but his stomach wasn't so sure. Ms. Marcus must've noticed.

"Grab the milk," she said. "I have bottles of water in my classroom. I'll put one in your cubby."

"Thanks," he said as he set the carton of milk on his tray.

"You sure you're not still sick?" she asked. "You look a little fishy."

The word *fishy* was too much for Raymond and he let out a laugh. But it jerked his stomach muscles and he immediately stopped.

"Sheesh, kid," Ms. Marcus said. "You better go put something in that stomach."

He nodded and made his way to an empty table where he ate his breakfast slowly.

Raymond checked his cubby before homeroom and in it

he found a bottle of water and a little Gatorade packet. He smiled and poured the powder into the water. He took a sip and instantly felt a little better. He wanted to thank Ms. Marcus but she was busy shuffling students to their seats to begin the day.

Raymond had stopped counting how many schools he had attended. Aside from being set farther from town, River Mill was no different from the rest. He had long since learned how to fly under the radar. How to stay invisible. He sat alone at lunch, usually reading or studying. He did not raise his hand in class if he could help it. He knew there would always be kids who wanted attention and there would always be others who were more than happy to give it to them. Raymond was neither. He did his work. He kept his mouth shut. This was how he had survived the children's home and this was how he had survived school after school.

Except there was one class in which Raymond was not as invisible as he would have liked. In art class, his new friend, Harlin, was the opposite of invisible. He talked nonstop and he was overly obsessed with cars. Most kids shook off their obsession with race cars before middle school, but not Harlin. And since he had lived in River Mill his whole life, all the kids knew who he was and knew *how* he was. He was loud. He talked with his mouth full and quite often without thinking first. Harlin attracted unwanted attention. And he was downright determined to be Raymond's friend. Raymond was finding it harder and harder to ignore him.

"You ever been to Hillsborough?" Harlin asked Raymond. He was cutting out a Maserati from a magazine ad and accidentally clipped a tire. "Dang it!" he shouted. "I heard they got a racetrack in Hillsborough that is so far back in the woods that you have to walk for a mile to get to it. Best-kept secret for drag-racers and racing rings. You ever heard of that? A racing ring is an illegal group of racers that bet money on races and switch locations to avoid the police." Harlin pronounced it *po-lice* like it was two different words.

Raymond was cutting out trees and he gave in. "How do the cars get there?" he asked.

"Whaddaya mean? They drive in," Harlin answered, rolling his eyes. "Don't you know how a car works?"

"No. I mean, yes, I know how a car works. I meant if it's back in the woods and you have to walk a mile to get to it, then how do they get the cars there?" He glued a tree to his paper.

Harlin looked stumped for a moment, then said, "Choppers. They chopper them in and drop 'em down on the track."

"Wouldn't the police notice if helicopters were carrying cars over the woods?"

"They do it at night," said Harlin, without missing a beat. Raymond quit trying.

"See ya tomorrow!" Harlin said to Raymond at the end of class.

"See ya," Raymond said. He milled around the crowd of kids in the bus lot and slipped into the woods unnoticed.

The dumpsters opened up a whole new world for Raymond. He had a food supply now, beyond what he could save from the cafeteria. But it required good timing on his part. He had to wait until dark and he couldn't seem to get the trash schedule down. That first week after finding the hollow, he either got there right after the trucks had emptied the dumpsters or way too late to find anything edible. Fish were also hard to come by. He had gone fishing almost every day and hadn't caught a single thing since that first brim. It had only been a short time, but Rosie was already visibly losing weight.

After science class the next day, Mr. Rosen asked Raymond to stay and help him clean up a lab before he went to lunch. Raymond carried the contents of the lab back to the supplies closet and stowed the boxes on the shelves. His stomach was growling, and he was eager to get to the cafeteria.

"Will you put that trash can back in the staff restroom on your way out?" Mr. Rosen asked, pointing to the small can by the door.

"Yes sir," Raymond said. He picked up the trash can and left the room. He opened the door to the staff restroom, flipped on the light, and set the trash can under the sink. He glanced in the mirror and turned to leave. There on the sink was an almost new bar of soap. Raymond hesitated. Then he wrapped the soap in a paper towel and tucked it in his bag. He hurried from the bathroom and checked the hall. It was empty. He exhaled and made his way to the cafeteria for lunch.

That afternoon, he stood on the sandy bank of the river, trying again to catch a fish. He had used every lure in his tackle box and nothing seemed to make a difference. Rosie was splashing around, trying to catch a minnow from a small school in the shallow water. Raymond thought he felt a tug on the line but it was a false alarm. He had just made up his mind to quit for the day when he noticed a dead minnow floating near Rosie. Rosie noticed too and began pawing at the minnow. She quickly got bored with this and abandoned the water altogether, deciding instead to take a nap in the sand.

Raymond set his fishing pole down and scooped up the tiny fish. There was no way he would eat another scavenged fish. But another fish might. It was worth a shot, he thought.

He pulled the line and cut the lure. He added weights and fastened a cork. Then he carefully secured the minnow to the hook. He cast the line and waited. After a few minutes he thought he felt a nibble. He reeled in the line. The minnow was still on the hook so he cast again. Finally, he felt the tug that he'd been waiting for and he jerked the line, setting the hook in the fish's mouth. He reeled in a small catfish and Rosie danced around at Raymond's feet.

So that was it. He couldn't fool these river fish with his lures. He must've just gotten lucky before. He walked to the edge of the water. There were a few more minnows swimming close to the bank. He tried to catch one, grabbing at the water, then felt silly. Of course he wouldn't catch a minnow like that. He tried inching his hand through the water slowly. They were just too fast. He needed a net.

That night, he and Rosie had catfish for dinner. It barely curbed his hunger, but it was better than nothing. It was another cold night and Raymond stayed by the fire until he ran out of sticks. Then he crawled into the cold hollow, holding his growling stomach. He tossed and turned, trying to ignore his hunger pains. He attempted to keep his mind occupied by thinking of ways he could make a net, but the cold kept winning out and he couldn't think clearly.

The next morning, Raymond woke up to a frost-covered earth and any thoughts of nets and fishing were pushed aside for thoughts of warmth. He shivered and cupped his hands to his face, trying to breathe life back into his stiff fingers. He had made his last gum-wrapper fire the night before.

Raymond sat through his classes thinking about how he could get a lighter or a box of matches. But he knew that he would have to walk into town to get either. And he didn't have any money. He needed more chewing gum wrappers. He tried looking through the trash but Ms. Marcus had caught him in the act. And although Raymond made up a story about accidentally throwing away his pencil, he wasn't sure Ms. Marcus believed him. He couldn't risk anyone else seeing him rummage through the trash during the school day.

In art, Harlin was raving on and on about his dad taking him to Commerce for his birthday in January when Raymond blurted out, "My birthday is tomorrow." It was a lie. Raymond's birthday was in June. But Harlin didn't know that.

"Well shoot!" said Harlin, unbothered by the interruption. "Your folks havin' a party or something?" Harlin had never been invited to a birthday party before, despite his many years of trying. Raymond's parents had never really celebrated birthdays except to remind him of how lucky he was to have two parents and a roof over his head. *Not so lucky now*, Raymond thought.

"Nah," said Raymond. "I'll probably just go fishing or something."

"Well what can I get you for your birthday?" asked Harlin. "A friend's gotta give his best buddy a birthday present."

The phrase *best buddy* weighed heavy on Raymond and he felt guilty for lying. But it was getting cold and he was running out of options.

"I don't need much," said Raymond. "Maybe just a few packs of chewing gum." He tried to avoid Harlin's eyes.

"Shoot, I'll do you one better than that!" Harlin said happily.

After school, Raymond headed back to the river, thinking again of minnows and catfish. He tried to use one of his T-shirts to scoop the minnows up, but the shirt was too heavy in the water and the minnows were too fast. He searched the woods for something that he could use to make a net. He found an old car tire, a flip-flop, and some empty soda bottles. He left the tire but picked up the sandal and the bottles to throw away later. He needed the minnows to catch fish, but all he kept finding was trash. He slept uneasily, hungry and shivering against the cold.

The next day, Harlin brought Raymond a big bag of candy, full of large-size chocolate bars, packs of SweeTARTS, and at least ten packs of chewing gum. "Happy birthday!" he said, thrusting the overflowing bag into Raymond's arms. "My gran works night shifts sometimes at the Shop-N-Save and gets to bring home the expired candy. But don't worry," he added, "it's still good. I eat it all the time."

"Thank you, Harlin," said Raymond. And Harlin grinned so big that Raymond thought the shame would eat him alive.

Chapter Seven

Even with the fresh stock of gum wrappers, Raymond nearly froze. He dug a small pit in the ground for his fire and circled it with larger rocks that he'd gathered from the woods. Though it lowered the visibility of the flames, he still didn't keep a fire going into the night. He was worried that somebody would see it through the trees, or worse, that he might set the woods on fire. There weren't any houses for at least a mile around the school. Raymond had checked. But cars still occasionally drove on the country roads at night. In that part of the county, it wasn't unusual for leftover brush fires or chimneys to burn into the night. But Raymond was careful. The last thing he wanted was to send up a smoke signal for someone to find him and drag him back to the children's home.

At breakfast on Friday, Harlin walked cheerily up to Raymond but was shoved into the table by an unknown assailant. The table jerked, spilling Raymond's milk and knocking over his neighbor's bottle of water. "Oof!" Harlin said. "Sorry about that. Must've tripped." Harlin brushed himself off and looked around. The boy who knocked into him was laughing with a friend as they left the cafeteria. Raymond hurried to clean up the spilled milk but Harlin didn't seem to notice. He sat down and stuffed his muffin into his mouth.

"You seen the Jamboree posters around?" Harlin asked, muffin falling from his mouth.

"Can't miss them," Raymond responded. The posters were everywhere. Raymond finished cleaning up the milk and helped clean the water across the table. Harlin picked the water bottle up from the floor but it was misshapen now so he stuck a finger through the mouth of the bottle, popping it back to its original form. Then he held it out to the kid sitting next to them. The kid looked incredulously at Harlin, rolled his eyes, and got up muttering something that didn't sound much like *thank you*. Harlin shrugged and set the bottle down. All of a sudden, Raymond remembered the minnows and it hit him. The bottle. He could use the empty bottles that he'd found to make traps for catching minnows.

After school, Raymond could hardly wait to get back to the hollow. He had three empty water bottles. He took out his fishing knife and cut off the top of one bottle. Then he flipped the top around so it looked like a funnel. He wedged the funnel into the bottom half of the bottle. It was so simple. He didn't need a net. He had everything he needed to make traps. He repeated the procedure on the other two bottles and then jogged to the river, traps in tow.

He found a few large rocks and used them to sink the traps and hold them in place under the water. He placed the traps along the bank where he had tried to catch minnows before. Now there wasn't anything to do but wait. Rosie nudged his leg.

"Hungry?" he asked her. He had been so excited about the

traps that he hadn't thought about saving food from breakfast or lunch. But now his stomach groaned. He wondered how long it would take to catch minnows. He checked the traps. They were empty. His stomach growled again and he decided to check the dumpsters.

The sun was setting but it was still light out when he reached the school. He checked the parking lots and they were empty of buses and cars. It was a Friday night and everyone had cleared out early, no doubt. Still, Raymond didn't want to risk being seen so he pulled himself up and into the dumpster. It had been a sunny day and the contents were smelly. He dumped out a bag and tried not to breathe through his nose. There was definitely nothing edible in there. He opened bag after bag and found more of the same. He made up his mind that he would just go back to the river and try his luck when he spotted a large silver can. He grabbed it, gagging at the trash that clung to it, and jumped from the dumpster.

He sucked in fresh air and wiped the can clean with his hand. It didn't have a label, but it was free of rust and dents so Raymond knew whatever was inside would probably be safe to eat. He walked back to camp and popped the top. Raymond had never been so excited to see Chef Boyardee in his life, family size and everything. He thought about making a fire to warm it up but he was too hungry. He ate sloppily, pouring the contents into his mouth. It wasn't spaghetti but it was just as satisfying. Rosie waited patiently for her portion, only whimpering the slightest bit. Raymond nodded through mouthfuls and dutifully shared half of the ravioli with her.

"Next time we'll warm it up first," he told Rosie. When they finished their dinner, Raymond washed up in the creek. His stomach wasn't quite as empty as before but it definitely wasn't full either. This seemed to be Raymond's new normal. Not quite starving but not exactly full. It was too dark to check the traps again tonight so Raymond built a fire and tried not to think about roasted fish.

He woke up early the next morning and immediately thought of the traps. He grabbed his fishing gear and walked to the river just as the sun was starting to rise. Rosie trotted along beside him. At the river, one of the traps had come loose and he found it floating near the bank. He bent to pick it up. It was empty. The second trap was half filled with sand but no minnows. Raymond's good mood vanished. It was soon lifted, though, by the contents of the third trap. Two minnows skirted the bottom of the bottle as Raymond lifted it from the river. He let out a yelp and punched the air.

The sun was up now. He put the empty traps back into the water, closer together this time, where the third trap had been. Then he set his two minnows down carefully and baited his hook. Raymond took a deep breath as he cast his line. This was good. He would be able to catch more fish now and Rosie would have more to eat. Now that he had a better chance of feeding her, he realized how worried he had been about it. He caught two fish in the first hour and cooked them, building a fire right there on the bank of the river. He checked his traps and found two more minnows. He baited his hooks and began roasting fish as he caught them. For the rest of the day, he repeated this process. He fished, cooked, and ate. He shared his catch with Rosie, who graciously accepted. Then at the close of the day, he stamped out the fire and walked back to camp with his first full belly in weeks. *I can do this*, he repeated to himself, and he was starting to really believe it.

On Sunday, Raymond walked through the woods with Rosie at his heels, gathering fallen limbs and dragging them back to camp. The trees were dense in this area and while it provided cover for Raymond, it also tended to keep things pretty wet if it rained. Raymond had learned that he could lay his kindling and firewood in a sunny spot to dry during the school day and then use the dried sticks to build a fire in the evening. But on the weekend, he found himself growing impatient, not wanting to wait all day or save wood in the evening. He decided to build a lean-to against the sunny side of the hollow to keep the moisture off his firewood. He vaguely remembered the field trip lesson on building shelters and thought he would at least give it a try.

When he had a pile of tree limbs, he set to work. He broke off any branches that stuck out from the larger limbs and tossed them in a pile until he had a small mountain of branches, each roughly an inch in diameter. He broke the ends from the branches to make them the same length and he did the same to the larger limbs by propping them against the tree and using the weight of his foot to break them in half. When he was satisfied, he began to weave the branches together, making a lattice pattern on the ground. Eventually, he had a wall of branches that he lifted up and propped against the side of the hollow. Some of them fell and he adjusted the weave or replaced them with another. It took him a few tries and he thought it could've looked a little neater but that didn't really matter.

Once the frame of the lean-to was against the tree, Raymond gathered smaller sticks and vines to weave in between the larger branches. It was time-consuming, tedious work and the sun was behind him before he knew it. He sat against the hollow, exhausted but feeling good. He hadn't finished but he had made a lot of progress. Rosie groaned and Raymond decided to give it a rest for the day.

"Let's get dinner, Rosie," he told her, and they headed to the river.

Chapter Eight

Raymond began to grow accustomed to his new routine. He would wake up, clean up around camp, slip into the crowd at the bus lot, and into the school. He would sit through his classes, listen to Harlin's endless chatter, and disappear back into the woods. He foraged for tree nuts, gathered sticks, did his homework while it was still light, and then fell asleep. He fished in the afternoons and used his fishing knife to whittle chunks of wood to pass the time. He used the empty ravioli can as a makeshift cup, scooping water from the creek and boiling it over his fire. The camp wasn't exactly home, but it worked. The more it worked, the more confident Raymond became in his ability to endure the winter: to survive in the woods behind his middle school. He tried to build fires only when needed, conserving his gum wrappers. And the shelter of the tree kept him dry on rainy nights. He finished the lean-to, weaving in so many sticks and vines that hardly any light passed through. Then he laid ferns and brush on top like a roof, hoping the moisture and rain would roll off.

He found a tree near the river with bark that peeled off like paper. It was so thin that Raymond could light it easily as tinder on the first try. This bark, Raymond thought, was made just for him. He called it a "paper tree" and had since found two more like it that kept his fires blazing without any trouble at all.

He used his bar of soap to clean himself and his clothes in the creek and occasionally, when he was sure he was alone, he would swim naked in the river, submerging himself in the cold water to rinse the dirt from his growing hair.

A kid in his math class made a comment about Raymond smelling like a campfire but he brushed it off and ignored it. Besides, it wasn't unusual for kids in this town to smell like a campfire.

He saw the same old man fishing on the other side of the river two more times but the man never offered more than a tip of his hat in Raymond's direction. Once, when Raymond caught a big bass, the man laughed a little at Rosie jumping for joy. It was the only thing he or the man had caught that day.

Raymond kept himself fed from the river, the school cafeteria, and his nighttime dumpster dives, occasionally finding unopened packs of crackers or Pop-Tarts. One night, he found an entire box of canned peaches. He ran back to the hollow, tripping over roots and branches. He opened a can and drank the juice first, savoring the sweet syrup before pouring the peaches into his mouth. He ate six cans in a row before forcing himself to stop and save the rest.

Some nights he would dream about his parents and wake up missing them. They were simple dreams mostly, like wishes that Raymond often said on his birthday each year. His mother would ask how his day was and make him an after-school snack. Or help him with his homework, something she had never done before but Raymond had seen mothers do on TV. In his dreams, his mother was kind and gentle, not at all like the hard, disengaged person she was in real life. Sometimes, after waking, he would lie there in the tree and wonder where they were. Did they miss him? Were they sorry? Would they ever come back? He tried to remind himself that he didn't need them, that he was fine without them. But he never quite believed himself. It wasn't all bad, living in the woods. Raymond liked the quiet and the freedom. Of course there were some things he couldn't help but miss. Like a bed. The tree hollow was as hard as stone and there were knots that stuck into Raymond's back. And a bathroom. Raymond had learned to adjust his bathroom schedule early on. He didn't mind going in the woods but it wasn't exactly ideal, and he definitely developed a new appreciation for toilets and running water. Still, it was better than the children's home.

Raymond sat with his eyes closed in Mr. Brewer's math class one morning. It was the warmest room in the building and he felt thawed out from the night before by the time class ended each morning.

It had been raining for days. What started as just a misting on Sunday gave way to a heavy, stinging rain that Raymond felt in his bones. When it finally ebbed, dark clouds hung low, blocking the sun. It made drying out a near impossibility. He had used almost an entire pack of gum trying to start a fire the night before and when he finally got one lit, the air was too wet to keep it going. He unwrapped leftover sandwich crusts for Rosie. Then he ate a Hershey bar from his stash and his last can of peaches, shivering in the cold of the hollow.

"Raymond!" Mr. Brewer yelled, jolting him awake. In the warmth of the room, Raymond had drifted off to sleep without realizing it.

Every set of eyes was on him now. "Sorry," he mumbled, cheeks hot.

"Is my class so boring to you that it puts you to sleep?" Mr. Brewer asked.

Raymond stared at his desk. He could feel the glares of his classmates burning into his skin. Most of these kids probably didn't even know his name until this very minute. "Well? Are you going to answer me?"

"No," Raymond choked out.

"No, you aren't going to answer me?"

Raymond flinched. "No, your class isn't boring."

"Well just to be sure, why don't you stand up for the rest of the class so you aren't tempted to doze off again."

Raymond looked up at Mr. Brewer and realized with horror that he was serious. He pushed his chair back, scraping it on the linoleum floor, and stood. He stared down at his desk. He could feel the heat in his throat as a lump swelled, threatening to explode. He swallowed hard. Raymond spent the rest of the class standing in the middle of the room while Mr. Brewer continued teaching as if nothing had happened. The lesson was on slope formulas but Raymond didn't hear any of it. He had broken the cardinal rule. He had gotten himself noticed. And once you are seen, there's no going back. Once you get noticed, it's like there's a spotlight that follows you wherever you go.

Raymond spent the rest of the day stiff with humiliation, imagining staring eyes following him through the hallways. Ms. Marcus passed out the latest Winter Jamboree flyer and assigned *The Outsiders* in English class but Raymond's mind was too clouded to concentrate.

He was relieved to sit down in art class where Harlin's constant talking distracted him from his previous humiliation.

"Man, I'd sure like to go to this NASCAR race," Harlin was saying.

"What NASCAR race?" Raymond asked.

Harlin was looking at the Winter Jamboree and Bingo Night flyer. Raymond leaned over to get a better look. The flyer advertised various games and prizes, including a pie-throwing contest and a raffle. But the majority of the flyer was taken up with the annual bingo game entry fees and prizes. The Jamboree was one week away and the bingo game would cost four dollars to enter and Raymond skimmed the list of prizes. A YETI cooler, an at-home spa kit, an autographed basketball, a thermal sleeping bag, tickets to a semi-professional NASCAR race in Commerce, gift baskets filled with themed goodies supplied by local businesses. Most of the items were of no interest to Raymond. But the sleeping bag caught his attention. The idea of a warm night's sleep was enough to make Raymond cry out with longing.

"Just four dollars," Raymond whispered.

"Yup!" said Harlin. "If I win those tickets to the race, I'll take you with me. I don't think my gran would mind."

Raymond gave Harlin a half smile. He considered asking Harlin if he could borrow the money but decided against it. "I guess your chances are as good as any," Raymond said. "I'd like that sleeping bag, myself."

"The sleeping bag?" asked Harlin, making a face. "Shoot, Ray, there's plenty of better prizes than that." Harlin had started calling Raymond "Ray" and although Raymond didn't care for the nickname that was also his father's, he didn't say anything about it. Harlin had turned out to be a good friend and Raymond still felt bad for lying to him about his birthday.

"I like to camp," Raymond said. And then quickly added, "But going to a race would be fun too."

"More than fun," Harlin said. "It'd be awesome! I wonder if Dale Earnhardt Jr. would be there. Not racing o' course, but maybe just there in the crowd. Maybe we would get to meet him and he could take us for a ride in his car."

Raymond didn't have the heart to tell Harlin that there was no way Dale Earnhardt Jr., or any other driver for that matter, would ever let Harlin get anywhere near their car. But he let him enjoy the fantasy.

"So, you're going to the Jamboree, then?"

"Shoot yeah," said Harlin. "Wouldn't miss it. Don't tell me you're thinking of missing it? Boy, it's going to be some kind of fun."

"I'll be there," said Raymond, still wondering how he could come up with the money.

"I heard about what happened in math," Harlin finally said, lowering his voice. It was obvious that he had been wanting to bring it up. The fact that he had held out this long made Raymond like him even more.

"Yeah," Raymond said, turning red around the ears.

"I had Mr. Brewer last year when he taught sixth grade. He's a jerk. Even *I* kept my mouth shut in that class."

"Yeah," Raymond said again, not wanting to relive his misery.

"It'll blow over," said Harlin, giving Raymond a stiff pat on the back. "Don't let it get to ya."

"Thanks," Raymond muttered. Eager to change the subject, he asked, "You reading *The Outsiders* for English?"

Harlin nodded. "We started it today. I don't really like reading all that much but the first chapter was good. I like the fighting."

"Yeah," said Raymond. He knew Harlin wouldn't care, but he didn't want to admit that he hadn't started reading it yet.

On the way out of school that day, Joseph Banker, the kid that had made paper footballs in Raymond's science class, shoved into him. "Watch it," he said. "Or are you sleepwalking now too?"

Raymond didn't say anything, stepping to the side to let Joseph go by. There was plenty of room to walk around him, but Joseph pushed his back as he walked past, causing Raymond to drop his things.

"Don't worry 'bout him," said Harlin, helping Raymond pick up his books and then jogging to keep up with him on the way to the bus lot. "He'll forget all about it by tomorrow." Raymond tried to smile. He hoped Harlin was right.

It felt like there were too many eyes on Raymond in the bus lot. His run-in with Mr. Brewer, and now Joseph, were obviously the only interesting things that had happened that day. He made up an excuse about forgetting something in his cubby and went back inside the school. This time, he left out the side door by the baseball field where nobody was around. When he was sure the coast was clear, he darted for the woods. He was almost to the tree line when a car turned into the side lot.

Raymond didn't know for sure if the driver had seen him but he didn't slow down to find out. He raced straight through the woods to the hollow and didn't turn around once.

Chapter Nine

When Raymond started reading *The Outsiders* that night, he really liked it. He liked that the boys in the book were on their own like he was. It made him feel a little less alone. He read the book by the light of the fire until he lost track of time. Ms. Marcus had only asked them to read the first two chapters but Raymond was halfway through it before he went to sleep that night.

At breakfast the next morning, Harlin asked Raymond to go to the school's basketball game with him that afternoon. River Mill was the only middle school in the county so when they had a game, it meant that a neighboring town was busing in a team, which didn't happen that often. The entire school was buzzing with excitement. Raymond had gotten to school early that morning and had studied the floors looking for change for the Winter Jamboree and all he had come up with was thirty-five cents.

"I need to find four dollars for the bingo entry," Raymond told Harlin. Raymond knew Harlin wouldn't ask him why he didn't ask his parents for the money. Harlin was a talker, but he hardly ever asked questions about Raymond's home life.

"Last year, I found a dollar bill under the bleachers after a game," Harlin said. "I always help Mr. Ingle with the cleanup after the games 'cause my gran can't pick me up till after her shift. Maybe you can find some change down there."

With the bingo game looming closer, Raymond figured it was worth a shot.

***

Almost every student at River Mill had gathered in the school's gymnasium for the game after school. Raymond and Harlin found empty spots in the bleachers and sat down to wait. Harlin was grinning from ear to ear and could hardly contain his excitement. To Raymond's horror, Joseph Banker and his cronies sat down in front of them.

"Well, well," Joseph said, sizing up Raymond and Harlin. "You two look like you came right out of the dumpsters." Raymond was instantly aware of the dirt stains on his hoodie.

"Find any good trash lately?" Jeremy Wallace, Joseph's constant companion, asked. "By the looks of your clothes, I'd say Christmas couldn't get here soon enough." Jeremy wasn't that smart but he was always well-dressed.

"Good one," Raymond muttered.

"Don't," Harlin whispered. "They ain't worth it." But Harlin's ears had turned a bright shade of red and he hunched over, trying to conceal the holes in his tattered blue jeans.

"I bet Christmas don't come at all by the looks of these two," said Joseph. "Your mom don't get around to shopping much from jail, does she?" He shoved Harlin's boot.

Raymond looked at his friend. Harlin hadn't mentioned anything about his mother being in jail. Harlin winced, obviously upset. He was staring at Joseph now. His smile had disappeared and his eyes blazed.

"Poor Harly," Joseph continued, using the voice that old ladies use when they talk to babies. "Mommy gone off to prison and Dad don't care enough to stick around."

Harlin's hands were shaking. "Shut up, Joseph," he said through gritted teeth.

"Whatsa matter, Harly?" Joseph asked, turning to face him. "Did you think nobody knew? My dad works for the police department and he told me that your mom ain't gettin' out for a long time. Robbed a convenience store. She probably don't even care. At least she gets to be away from you. Worth shooting a—" But Joseph never got a chance to finish his sentence. Harlin jumped up and punched him right in the eye with a resounding *POP!*

Joseph fell from the bleachers and scrambled to get up. Harlin was on top of him in a second. And then Mr. Brewer was there, grabbing Harlin by his shirt collar, dragging him off Joseph. Raymond jumped up to protest.

"Joseph was talking about Harlin's mom!" Raymond yelled, but Mr. Brewer didn't wait to hear the whole story.

"You!" he said, pointing at Raymond. "And you!" He pointed at Joseph, who was cupping his face and whimpering.

"He just hit me for no reason," Joseph whined. "I didn't say anything to him. Ask anyone." Joseph's friends were nodding but silent. The whole gymnasium had quieted down, eagerly watching the scene.

"That's not true," Raymond yelled, furious at the indignity. Harlin looked crestfallen. He was limp like he had turned to jelly in Mr. Brewer's grip. He stared at the gym floor as silent tears fell from his face. It was the longest time Harlin had gone without talking in all the time Raymond had known him.

Mr. Brewer kept a firm grip on Harlin's shirt collar as he dragged him from the gymnasium toward the front office. Raymond and Joseph walked silently behind them. Raymond was fuming. Joseph was moaning and whimpering over his eye, which had already begun to turn purple. When they reached the office, Mr. Brewer dropped Harlin in a chair outside the principal's office and shoved the other two boys inside. He explained what he had seen to Mrs. Harding, the school principal, while Raymond listened, furious.

Since this was the boys' first offense, Mrs. Harding went easy on them and only suspended Harlin from school for the rest of the week. She banned all three of the boys from attending any River Mill athletics events for the rest of the season. Raymond and Joseph sat in silence across her desk, staring at the floor.

"I'm very disappointed in you," she told Raymond. "Ms. Marcus says you are one of her brightest students. Bright students don't get wrapped up in fights." It wasn't fair. Joseph was the one who deserved to be punished, not Harlin.

"Harlin was defending himself," Raymond said angrily. "Joseph was the one egging him on, talking about his mother." He felt like it was his duty as Harlin's friend to set the story straight. He knew Harlin would do the same for him. He braved a glance at Mrs. Harding.

Mrs. Harding was a formidable woman. She wore her hair in a tight bun and held her shoulders back with her arms crossed in front of her. Raymond saw her hard face falter for a moment. "Harlin has had a rough go," she said. "But that doesn't excuse his behavior." Her tone was calmer now. "You can't go around punching someone, even if it is well-deserved." She eyed Joseph.

"I'll have to call your parents," Mrs. Harding said, and Raymond's heart dropped to the floor. Before he could protest, Mrs. Harding added, "You can go, Raymond."

"So you aren't calling my parents?" Raymond asked.

"No," said Mrs. Harding, taking a long look at him. "You weren't the one fighting, Raymond. But I never want to hear about you even stepping one foot out of line again, or I will."

"Yes ma'am," Raymond said, jumping up. He couldn't get out of the office fast enough. He left Joseph sitting there as Mrs. Harding picked up the phone.

Harlin was on a bench just outside of Mrs. Harding's office. "Hey," Raymond said.

"Hey," said Harlin without looking up. He sat staring at his hands. He looked like someone had told him NASCAR was canceled for the year. "You ain't in trouble, are you?" he asked, looking up at Raymond.

Raymond lowered his voice. "Nah. Only a telling off. It was worth it, though, to see the look on Joseph's face when you slugged him."

Harlin tried to smile but his face fell. "My gran's gonna be so mad."

"She'll understand," Raymond said. Harlin shook his head. Raymond didn't want to leave him there alone but he didn't want to hang around for Mrs. Harding to change her mind about calling his parents. "I'd better get going. The rest of the week will fly by, Harlin, and you'll be back to school before you know it."

"Yeah. See ya, Ray." Harlin met Raymond's eyes for a moment and then looked away again, staring back at his bruised hand.

Raymond felt helpless. He wished that he could've done more to help. Harlin didn't deserve any of this. It was Joseph who should be suspended, not Harlin.

Back in the woods, Raymond's emotions finally got the better of him. He kicked leaves and scattered his stick pile. He kicked the side of the wide tree trunk that was his home, pretending it was Joseph's face. "Ow!" he hollered, jumping up and down on one foot, clutching the toe of his shoe. He collapsed into a pile of brush. It wasn't fair. None of it was fair. His parents leaving. Living in a tree. Harlin's mom in jail. Angry tears poured down Raymond's face. Rosie crept over and nestled her head under his arm.

A few minutes passed before Raymond got up and started picking up the sticks that he had scattered. He threw them angrily back into a pile. "No fire tonight," he snapped at Rosie. "There's a basketball game. Someone might see." He chucked one of the sticks into the woods, pulled his hoodie over his mouth, and screamed into it.

It was another cold night. Raymond layered on all the clothes he owned and wrapped an arm around Rosie in the hollow of the tree. He felt bad for yelling at her. He was exhausted but wide awake at the same time. He tried to occupy his mind with other ways that he could come up with the money to play bingo, but all he could think about was Joseph Banker. Joseph's mother was probably doctoring his black eye at that very moment while Joseph moaned that it wasn't fair. Raymond gritted his teeth and held Rosie tighter.

That night, he dreamed that he was the one with all the friends and that his own mother had marched up to the school and demanded to know what had happened to her son. She made him spaghetti for dinner and held frozen peas on his black eye while they watched TV together. Then he had gone to sleep in a king-size bed with the biggest, fluffiest comforter wrapped around him.

Raymond woke up to the cold tree hollow. With the dream fresh in his mind, he swore under his breath. Rosie flinched. He dragged himself up and wiped the dust from his gray hoodie. He changed his clothes and stomped toward the school without so much as a backward glance at his dog.

He ate breakfast alone, wrapping his leftover biscuit in a napkin. He felt a pang of regret for how he left Rosie. None of this was her fault. Now on top of being frozen and angry, he had to feel guilty too. He threw the Styrofoam tray in the trash with force and shoved his hands in his pockets. He made his way through the cafeteria and pushed through the door. He wasn't paying attention as he walked and he slammed into someone. Books scattered to the floor.

"Watch where you're going!" he snapped.

"Sorry, Raymond," a hurt voice said. It was Lexi, the redhead from his science class.

"Oh. Sorry, Lexi," Raymond said, his tone changing from annoyance to apology. "I didn't see you."

"Are you okay?" Lexi looked from Raymond to the books strewn across the floor.

"Ye-a-h," he stammered, backing away from her. "Really sorry." He turned and continued down the hall, leaving Lexi to gather her spilled books alone.

At his cubby, Raymond shook his head in frustration and gathered his things for math. Harlin was suspended. He had snapped at Rosie, and now he had managed to bump into the only other person who had been nice to him at River Mill. He admonished himself for not helping her pick up her things. Couldn't he get anything right?

Students were shuffling into the classroom, grabbing their books, and chatting excitedly. He heard a few whispers about the fight but mostly they were talking about the basketball game.

"Raymond," Ms. Marcus called. "Come here, please."

Raymond walked over to his teacher. She was sitting at her desk, clicking away at the keys on her computer. She looked up as he approached, a concerned expression on her face.

"Are you all right, Raymond? I heard about what happened yesterday."

"Yes ma'am," Raymond said flatly, not wanting to discuss the incident.

He thought Ms. Marcus was going to give him a lecture on fighting but instead, she said, "That Joseph Banker is nothing but trouble. You stay away from him, Raymond. You're too smart to get wrapped up in his drama. And you tell Harlin," she continued, "not to worry one minute about what other people say. Folks around here can't ever seem to mind their own business."

Raymond was surprised. He didn't know what to say so he just nodded.

"Everything else okay, Raymond?" she asked. "I've noticed your grades have been slipping a little. Are you able to study at night?"

Ms. Marcus seemed genuinely concerned. Raymond wanted to tell her that he wasn't able to study because he was busy trying not to starve and freeze to death every night. But he remembered the last time a teacher tried to help him and what that had gotten him.

"Is there anything I can—"

"Everything is great," Raymond said, cutting her off. "We've just been busy at home lately with the holidays coming."

Ms. Marcus sighed. "Okay, Raymond. Let me know if you need anything, all right? Anything at all."

Later on, in math class, Mr. Brewer didn't mention the events from the day before. In fact, he didn't speak to Raymond at all. They had a quiz at the beginning of class and then a short review. When he was finished with the lesson, Mr. Brewer gave them directions for practice problems and sat down at his desk. Raymond opened his math book and stared down at it. There was a crisp five-dollar bill lying on the inside cover.

Chapter Ten

The Winter Jamboree was scheduled for the last night before Christmas break. Then the school would be closed until the new year. Raymond would be on his own for a total of thirteen days and fourteen nights. Raymond tried to prepare as best he could. He was careful not to eat the sealed packages and cans that he found in the dumpster, tucking them in the back of the hollow for safekeeping. He still had four candy bars and three packs of gum left from Harlin. He could only hope that they would last until school was back in session. He knew that if he could catch fish in the river, which had proven difficult lately with the cold weather, he would be all right. He had attempted to insulate the hollow, hanging ferns over the opening, sewing them together with the string of his hoodie. He padded the inside of the hollow with more ferns and with dried leaves and pine straw. It didn't do much to warm him, but he was at least grateful to be shielded from the sometimes bitter cold winds that blew throughout the night.

When he had gotten back to the hollow that day after finding the money, it had taken Rosie a while to forgive his shortness from earlier. Finding the money had pushed all thoughts of the fight from Raymond's mind and he was sorry for how he had treated Rosie that morning.

She had been lying in a patch of sunlight when he arrived.

"Hey, Rosie," Raymond greeted her. But Rosie just stared at him. "Come here, girl," Raymond called. Rosie looked at him for a few seconds and then turned and began cleaning her paws, ignoring him. Raymond sighed. He sat down next to her and gingerly stroked her head and back. "I'm sorry. I was a jerk." Rosie allowed him to rub her belly, stretching her legs out. Raymond laughed and she licked his cheek. After he'd been forgiven, he stretched out in the sunlight next to his dog. He had held the five-dollar bill out in front of him, thinking of who could've given it to him. It couldn't have been Harlin because he was suspended when Raymond found the money. He thought it had to have been Ms. Marcus because his cubby was in her room. But how would she know that he needed money? Raymond had only told Harlin and he was sure Harlin wouldn't have told anyone. If someone knew that he needed money, what else did they know?

Raymond resolved to be more careful. He couldn't have anyone snooping around or paying too close attention to him. In the days that followed the fight, Raymond was extra careful about sneaking into the woods. He began walking down the road after school like he was walking to his old trailer and when no cars were coming, he would jump into the woods and backtrack to the hollow.

When Harlin's suspension ended, Raymond was eager to find his friend in the cafeteria and tell him about the money. He wondered if Harlin might know something about who had given it to him. But before Raymond could sit down at the table, Harlin was already talking.

"Man, am I happy to see you! My gran wouldn't let me out of the house. Said I was grounded and gave me a list of chores to do every day. She had me cleaning toilets and doing laundry. I swear, I've never been much for school but I couldn't wait to get back here. She made me regrout the bathroom floor. Do you know how hard it is to—"

"Harlin," Raymond broke in, "did you put a five-dollar bill in my math book?" Harlin hadn't talked to anyone but his gran in a week and Raymond didn't know when he would come up for air.

Harlin looked confused. "Did I—" He broke off. "No. Someone gave you five dollars? Well, that's great, Raymond! Now you can play the bingo game at the Jamboree tomorrow night."

Raymond lowered his voice to a whisper. "Yeah it's great and all, but are you sure it wasn't you?"

"I'm sure. Shoot if I had an extra five dollars, I wouldn't be giving it to you. No offense, o' course."

"Right," said Raymond. Then it wasn't Harlin. He sat back in his chair.

"Who do ya think gave it to you?" Harlin asked. Raymond shrugged. If it wasn't Harlin, then it had to be Ms. Marcus. She was the one who had given him the toothpaste, after all. Hadn't she? He had assumed it was her but now he thought maybe he was wrong about that too. The whole thing made Raymond nervous. He considered turning the money in to the office and saying he found it somewhere. But the days had only grown colder and the nights were worse. Raymond needed that sleeping bag.

"Raymond?" Harlin said, breaking into Raymond's thoughts.

"Yeah?"

"I asked you if you wanted to meet up before the Jamboree tomorrow? My gran is working but she said she would drop me here on her break."

"Oh. Sure," said Raymond. He was still lost in thought but Harlin didn't seem to mind. He continued to talk all through breakfast. In art class, he picked up right where he left off, never giving Raymond a chance to respond. But Raymond didn't mind. He was busy thinking about the money and the Jamboree. He now had enough money to buy into the bingo game. He just needed to win. He wished it was something other than bingo. At least then he could have practiced or prepared. There was no preparing for a bingo game. You were either lucky or you weren't.

Raymond's teachers didn't seem to notice that the Christmas holiday was approaching. It seemed to Raymond that they were assigning more homework than ever. Mr. Brewer had assigned math questions every night and Raymond had to keep the fire going much later than he was comfortable with just so he could see the problems in the book. He had finished *The Outsiders* already so at least Ms. Marcus might give him a break in English. Even Mr. Rosen asked the students to choose a science fair project over the break. Raymond had to prioritize the light, waking up early to complete his work instead of working into the night. His grades weren't the best they'd ever been and he sometimes forgot all about assignments, letting his hunger take priority. Still, he wasn't failing and that would have to be enough.

The following night, Raymond waited for Harlin just inside the gymnasium entrance. There were kids everywhere. There was a cotton candy station, game booths with prizes, a bouncy house that cost fifty cents a turn, and pizza for a dollar a slice.

When Harlin got there, he and Raymond walked through the unrecognizable school gym admiring the games and watching the other kids throw darts at balloons or try to guess how many jelly beans were in a jar. Raymond spent his spare dollar on a slice of pepperoni pizza, pocketing the other four. He wrapped the crust and pepperonis in a napkin for Rosie.

The pie-throwing booth was set up near the back exit of the gymnasium. Raymond saw Mr. Brewer wiping whipped cream off his face and laughing. Raymond wished he had saved his extra dollar to throw a pie at Mr. Brewer. Joseph was cleaning up the fallen pie remnants. He was still sporting a black eye and he glowered at Raymond and Harlin as they walked past.

In the school auditorium, Raymond and Harlin bought their bingo boards, and found two empty seats together at the front, closest to the prize table. The prizes were organized neatly with the autographed basketball and the pair of NASCAR tickets up front. The sleeping bag was at the far end of the table and Raymond looked at it longingly.

"You must really like camping," Harlin said, watching Raymond eye the sleeping bag.

"What? Oh yeah." Raymond nodded. And then before he could think better of it, he blurted out, "I need that sleeping bag, Harlin."

"If you say so," Harlin said, shrugging.

He examined his game board. *Please,* he thought. *Please be a winner.*

"Hey, Raymond," a cheerful voice said from beside him. He looked to his right. He had sat down next to Lexi without realizing it. How had he missed her red hair?

"Hi, Lexi." Raymond smiled. He still felt bad about leaving her to pick up her books that day in the hall, but he was too embarrassed to apologize.

"Ready to play?" she asked happily. One of Lexi's friends leaned forward to see who she was talking to. She smiled and looked past Raymond. "Hey, Harlin," the friend said. Harlin's eyes grew to the size of golf balls. His face turned bright red, and he opened his mouth to say something but then he shut it again quickly. Another girl sat down on the other side of them and Lexi and her friend turned to say hello. Raymond smiled.

"Cat got your tongue, Harlin?" he asked quietly, laughing at his friend.

"Aw shut it," said Harlin.

When the bingo game began, a round woman with big hair and too much makeup went over the rules. She instructed everyone to grab one of the erasable markers from the basket on each table. And then she called the first combination. Raymond was anxious and sweaty. His hands shook as he marked B5 on his game board.

Six combinations were called before someone in the back yelled "Bingo!" And the autographed basketball was taken from the table. Raymond felt sick as he wiped his board clean with an eraser. He tried to focus on the spinning balls up front, willing them to spit out the right combinations.

The woman called, "B12!" and Raymond anxiously marked his board again.

"Bingo!" a man yelled from the back after the seventh spin. Raymond breathed a sigh of relief as the YETI cooler disappeared and they were instructed to clear their boards.

The woman began a new game, pulling ball after spinning ball. After N34 and N40 were both called without incident, the woman spun the basket, pulled a ball, and announced "O67!"

"Bingo," a shocked voice whispered next to Raymond. Harlin was staring at the game board. He blinked a few times and shouted happily, "Bingo!" He slowly pushed his chair out and walked to the front. He picked up the envelope with the two NASCAR tickets inside and held it gingerly.

"Congratulations, young man!" the woman said cheerily and then reminded everyone that there were still all kinds of prizes left for the taking. Harlin sat back down slowly, staring at the tickets.

"Congratulations, Harlin," Lexi said.

Harlin looked up, dazed. "Thanks!" The corner of his mouth finally turned up in a half-stunned grin. Raymond started bouncing his legs up and down under the table.

The woman continued up front, calling combination after combination. Raymond's hands were shaking. "G52!" she announced.

And before Raymond could mark the spot that put him one combination away from the sleeping bag, an excited voice yelled, "Bingo!" from the end of Raymond's table. The boy was small, even smaller than Raymond, and the man to his right, who could only be his father, clapped him on the back as he stood to claim his prize. Raymond watched as the boy paced the table, unsure of what to take. Then he stopped at the end of the prizes and picked up the green flannel sleeping bag. He held it over his head in triumph as his dad whooped.

Raymond sat frozen. He watched the boy walk away with his only chance at a warm winter. The familiar lump in his throat was back and he could feel the tears coming. Harlin said something next to him but Raymond didn't hear. He set down his ink marker, pushed the chair from the table, and walked out of the auditorium, leaving his friend to stare after him.

He made his way to the bathroom and locked the stall door behind him. He sat alone on the cold porcelain. He rubbed his knuckles together as tears fell onto his hands. What was he going to do now? He had pinned all his hopes on winning that sleeping bag and now that it was over, he thought of how cold the next few months would be. He cursed himself for buying a slice of pizza when he could've used that money on a lighter or a box of matches. He stayed in the bathroom until the Jamboree was over. A man came in to clean and told him they were locking up.

Raymond headed down the hall to the exit. Most of the people were gone now, leaving a few parents and school volunteers to pack up the game booths and haul trash bags out to the dumpsters. Harlin was waiting outside for his grandma to pick him up.

"Hey," said Raymond.

"Hey, Ray, where'd you get off to?" Harlin asked.

"I just needed a minute," said Raymond. "Congrats on winning the tickets, Harlin. I know how much you wanted them."

Harlin leaned over to pick something up. Raymond hadn't noticed the flannel sleeping bag at Harlin's feet. He handed it to Raymond. "It seemed like you really wanted this so I traded it for the NASCAR tickets."

Raymond didn't know what to say. Harlin was obsessed with NASCAR. Nobody had ever done anything like this for Raymond.

"Harlin, I . . ." Raymond started.

Harlin shrugged. "My gran woulda never let me go to that race anyway. It's too far away, and she complains about just having to drive me to school sometimes. Anyway, I know how much you wanted that sleeping bag. Maybe we can go camping together sometime?"

"I'd like that," said Raymond. Still clutching the soft flannel in his arms, he added, "Thank you, Harlin. You're a good friend." Right then, an old hatchback pulled up and the driver honked the horn, making Raymond jump.

"That's my gran," said Harlin. "I'll see ya in a couple of weeks. Merry Christmas!"

"Merry Christmas," Raymond said, and he watched his friend get into the car and drive away. He walked to the edge of the school and slipped into the shadows. He made his way by moonlight back to the hollow and found Rosie lying in the leaves.

"Look what we got, girl," he said, leaning down to stroke her fur. Rosie nudged the sleeping bag with her nose and wagged her tail. Raymond laid the leftover pizza crust and pepperonis by her head and rolled the sleeping bag into the length of the fallen tree. He crawled in, feeling the warmth of the flannel. Even the blankets at his parents' weren't as nice as this.

A cold rain had started to fall and Raymond propped himself up, looking out at it. Rosie jumped in beside him and curled up at the opening of their new bed. It was the first time Raymond had felt relaxed in weeks, maybe longer. As the rain pattered outside, he drifted slowly off to sleep.

Chapter Eleven

In the early hours of the morning, the temperature dropped and the rain turned to snow. When Raymond woke up, he lay with his eyes closed, relishing the warmth of his new bed. Rosie was asleep next to him. He reluctantly opened his eyes and pulled himself out of the sleeping bag, trying not to wake her. He put on his hoodie, zipped his coat over it, and slipped on his shoes. Outside of the hollow, he stretched and shivered, his muscles protesting against the cold. Raymond ate a Pop-Tart for breakfast. Rosie woke up at the sound of the wrapper and Raymond offered her the unfrosted edges. He brushed his teeth at the creek and grabbed his fishing gear. Rosie whined but jumped from the hollow and followed him into the falling snow.

He checked his minnow traps and pulled a single minnow from the bottle. There was no sign of the man at the river but Raymond thought that most people probably don't go fishing when it was snowing out. Then again, most people didn't live in hollowed-out trees behind their middle school either.

After a few hours, Raymond was wet from head to toe and his legs ached from cold. Rosie had given up scavenging in the snow, which was now sticking to the frozen earth. She was curled at the base of a wide rock, covered in snow, with her nose tucked under her legs. Raymond alternated hands. He had hoped to catch at least one fish, but so far he hadn't had so much as a bite. The clouds hung low and the snow fell in heavy thumb-size flakes, clinging to Raymond's hair and clothes. He thought of the warm new sleeping bag and pulled in his line.

"Come on, Rosie," he called, and she happily jumped up and shook the snow from her fur. As Raymond knelt to close his tackle box, the hairs on the back of his neck prickled. He'd had this feeling before. Like he was being watched. He turned but he could barely see through the thick snowfall. Raymond stood and squinted, scanning the woods around him. Rosie yipped impatiently. He decided the cold must be getting to him. He picked up his things and followed after her, glancing over his shoulder again before the river was out of sight.

At the hollow, he took his wet clothes off and stuffed them at the back of the tree, shivering in the cold. He pulled on dry pants and a T-shirt and zipped himself into the sleeping bag, letting Rosie slide in next to him. He had checked out a copy of the *Boy Scouts Handbook*, hoping it would come in handy. He thumbed the pages before casting it aside. He reached for his fishing knife and began to whittle down a small log that lay at the mouth of the hollow. Raymond had grown very good at this over the last few weeks, passing the time by making small wooden statues of squirrels and fish that he lined up at the back of the hollow. There was even one of Rosie. Today, his stiff fingers struggled to hold the small knife. Eventually, he cast the log aside too and tucked the knife away. It was just too cold and there wasn't enough light in the hollow to see properly anyway.

The next morning, Raymond woke up to an empty tree.

He could hear Rosie outside and he pulled himself to the edge of the hollow to call for her. It had stopped snowing in the night, leaving behind at least three inches of powder. Rosie had a freshly dead squirrel in her mouth. She dropped it at the base of the tree and proudly looked up.

"Okay, girl," Raymond said. "I get it." She was too skinny, unable to eat the fruit and chocolate that Raymond so often had available. He grabbed the discarded handbook and checked the index. To his extreme dismay, he couldn't find anything about skinning animals or cooking game. He resolved to try anyway. "Can't be that hard, right?"

He retrieved a smooth stone he had collected from the river. He sharpened his knife on the stone before he began the work of skinning the animal. Raymond remembered watching a few episodes of a survival show with his dad a long time ago where the contestants had to skin a mink. A squirrel was a little smaller than a mink but it couldn't be that different. He tried to steady his hands. After accidentally slicing the tail of the squirrel clean off, he wedged the knife underneath the skin at the tailbone, slowly pulling it back. It took him a few tries but he managed to pull the skin from the squirrel without many mishaps. He cut off the head and sliced the belly, taking care to remove the entrails without spoiling the meat. Feeling quite accomplished, he skewered the animal with the stick he used to roast fish and held it over the fire.

He and Rosie ate squirrel for breakfast. It wasn't the best-tasting thing Raymond had ever eaten, but it also wasn't the worst. "Get a few more like that, Rosie, and we'll have ourselves a Christmas feast," he told her, and laughed. His stomach wasn't even close to being full but his spirits were up. Rosie licked his face in agreement.

On the survival show, the man who skinned the mink had gotten very sick with E. coli and had to be sent home. Raymond couldn't remember if it was from the meat or not. But he remembered he was sent home because Raymond's father had gotten so upset about it that he had thrown a bottle at their TV. The TV didn't break but there was a bright spot in the middle of the screen after that. If a character on-screen moved near the bright spot, they would momentarily disappear and then reappear when they moved away again. He stared up into the canopy of frosted trees and and patted Rosie's head.

After breakfast, Raymond put out the fire, grabbed his fishing pole, and headed back out to the river. He figured if Rosie could have such good luck, maybe he could too.

On the way, Raymond marveled at the snow-covered woods. Everything looked so different covered in white. It was quieter than usual. Most of the birds had gone for the winter, in search of warmer climates. They were almost to the river when Raymond stopped. He had the feeling again that some-one was watching him. Rosie stopped next to him. Raymond looked around, trying to control his breath, which was now coming in quick, sharp pulls. Somewhere to his right, a tree branch snapped and crashed to the ground, heavy with snow. Raymond jumped. Then relaxing a bit, he smiled at Rosie. "I think the woods are getting to us."

But Rosie was staring straight ahead, hackles raised. Raymond followed her gaze. A coyote was standing just ten yards ahead, blocking their path to the river. Raymond sucked in his breath, feeling the cold air rush into his lungs. Panic surged through his body. The coyote didn't move. He was looking right at them. Then he took a small step forward and Raymond watched his shoulder blades lift, hot breath making smoke clouds in the air. Rosie emitted a low shaking growl that Raymond had never heard from her before.

The coyote took another step. Raymond searched his brain for anything he could remember about coyotes. He had heard stories of them preying on small children or eating family pets. Despite the cold, sweat beaded on his forehead and ran down his neck. His heart was beating out of his chest. Coyotes were stalking animals. Raymond forced his feet to move toward the beast, taking a step forward and fighting every impulse in his body to run as fast as he could in the opposite direction.

The coyote stopped, shifting his eyes from the dog to the boy. His head tilted and his tail twitched. Then he lifted his head and let out an earsplitting yowl that made Raymond jump and scream out. Rosie leaped in front of Raymond, teeth bared.

In an instant, the coyote was bounding through the snow, straight for them. Raymond dropped his fishing gear and tried to run. He made it about six paces before falling face forward into the snow. He could hear the coyote and Rosie wrestling behind him. He flipped himself over quickly, shuffling back.

He had to blink several times to adjust to the sight that lay before him.

The coyote was bouncing around Rosie, running in circles and jamming his nose into the dog, who was still frozen to the ground, hackles raised, growling, and snapping at his advances. The coyote turned and ran a figure eight in the opposite direction, running at full speed back to where Rosie stood. He slid into her, leaned his head down under her small frame, and threw her easily into the air.

Rosie sailed through the air and thumped into the snow. She rolled onto her side just as the coyote leaped over her. He darted back, circling her again. He wasn't attacking, Raymond thought, stunned. He was *playing*. Raymond sat in the snow, mouth open, watching the ridiculous dance of the bounding ginger beast.

Rosie was no longer growling but she was obviously beyond irritated. She snapped at the coyote, who was jumping over her with ease. He was at least twice her size. Raymond didn't know what to do. He got to his feet, suddenly aware of the wet cold that was permeating the bottoms of his jeans. The coyote halted and swung his head in Raymond's direction. Raymond wasn't sure if his playfulness would extend to humans and before he could think better of it, he took a few steps back.

The coyote bounded toward him, his great tongue hanging out of his open mouth. With two leaps, he closed the distance between himself and Raymond. Raymond closed his eyes and braced for impact but it never came. When he opened them again, Rosie had her mouth clamped around the coyote's ankle, dragging him away from Raymond. The coyote kicked out and Rosie released him, yelping in pain, falling into the snow.

"Rosie!" Raymond screamed out, and he ran to her. Her right leg was twisted awkwardly under her. Raymond positioned himself protectively over his dog, leaning low and soothing her. She tried to get up and yelped again in pain.

Raymond looked up at the beast, who was still waiting eagerly, tail wagging. "Go!" Raymond yelled. Fear left him and he was suddenly furious. He stood and waved his arms at the coyote. "Get out of here!" He grabbed a handful of snow and flung it at the animal. The coyote backed up but made no move to leave. Raymond screamed again, a guttural sound even he didn't know he could make. He scooped up his dog and ran back in the direction of the hollow, leaving the coyote behind in the snow-covered woods.

By the time he made it back to the hollow, he was soaked from snow and sweat. He laid Rosie gently in the mouth of the tree and bent over her, assessing the damage.

"It's all right, girl. I've got you." She had been quiet while Raymond carried her but whimpered now, licking her hurt leg. Raymond touched it and she pulled it away from him. "Let me see it, Rosie." The leg didn't appear to be broken but the skin just above the paw was badly bruised and split open, already swelling. Rosie tried to stand, crying out as she applied weight to it. Raymond tried to keep his voice steady. "Shh. Stay down now," he whispered. His thoughts were hazy and he began to shake uncontrollably. He grabbed the *Boy Scouts Handbook* and flipped to the index. His fingers trembled as he turned page after page in search of a remedy. He scanned the sections on sprains and splints. He wasn't sure if the paw was sprained, though, or simply bruised. There wasn't anything about wound care of animals. He threw the book into the snow.

"We have to clean it up." He knew that much. He tried to gather the dog in his arms again and she protested, flailing back. "We have to clean it!" he yelled, adrenaline still coursing through him. Rosie whined but gave in, allowing him to carry her to the small creek. He knelt by the water and laid her in the snow, carefully scooping water onto the cut. Rosie struggled to pull her leg away. Raymond leaned against her, applying just enough pressure to keep her still. "Good girl, Rosie," he whispered. "Good girl." He doctored the bleeding cut with cold water until he felt that it was clean. Then he carried her back to the hollow and laid her gently on the sleeping bag.

The sun was out now, sneaking through the bare branches of the trees. For the rest of the day, Raymond tried to keep himself busy. Every couple of hours, he pulled Rosie to the front of the hollow and packed snow around the swollen paw. It had doubled in size since the morning but the bleeding had stopped. Rosie tried to lick the cut and Raymond had to stay on her to keep her from overdoing it. As the sun set, Raymond grew increasingly worried. He hadn't eaten since the squirrel and his stomach growled in protest. His body ached from the day's events as he tucked himself into the sleeping bag. He wrapped his arms around his dog and said a silent prayer that she would be okay. She had to be okay.

Chapter Twelve

The following day, Rosie's paw was swollen to the size of an orange and she didn't protest when Raymond pulled himself out of the sleeping bag, trying to ease around her. He pulled a can of shredded chicken from the back of the hollow. He had found it on a particularly good scavenging day and was saving it for a special occasion. He felt Rosie needed it now more than ever. And then, realizing that his fishing gear that held the small knife that he used to open cans was in the woods by the river, he threw the can out of the hollow's opening and into the snow. The coyote jumped to avoid it.

"You!" Raymond yelled. "You get out of here!" He jumped from the tree. He instantly wished he had put on his shoes. "Get out of here!" he yelled again but the coyote just looked at him. "You hurt her! You hurt her and now she can't even walk! What are we going to do now, huh? What are we going to do?" He flung his hands into the snow, wildly throwing handfuls toward the animal.

The coyote stretched his legs in front of him and lay down. Raymond stared at him, trying to catch his breath. He needed to get back to the river and get his fishing gear but he wasn't about to leave Rosie there alone with the coyote lurking around their camp. Friendly as he seemed, Raymond didn't trust the animal.

He grabbed a dry pair of socks and his tennis shoes, still damp from the day before. Then, eyeing the coyote, he climbed back into the hollow to gather Rosie up. "Come on," he whispered. "We have to go back and get the knife." Rosie arched away, laying her head back on the sleeping bag. Raymond screamed and punched the inside of the tree, crying out in pain. He slumped against the hollow. His stomach groaned. He pulled a pack of crackers from his stash and offered Rosie a square. She licked it and then laid her head down, uninterested. Raymond forced himself to eat the remaining crackers, looking from Rosie to the coyote. Then he pulled himself back out of the hollow and began building a fire. The coyote watched as he stacked the sticks, using two bigger logs at the base. He had gotten good at catching the spark of the gum wrapper with dry leaves and lit the fire on the first try.

After a while, it was steady enough to add wet sticks, drying them out until they too burned down. Using wet sticks created more smoke, but Raymond didn't have a choice. He perched himself on a log and removed his damp shoes, letting the fire dry them out.

The coyote stuck around all day, watching Raymond putter about the camp and pack Rosie's paw in snow. The paw wasn't getting any better but it also didn't look any worse. Raymond was quietly thankful for that. Rosie kept trying to lick the wound and Raymond ran back and forth from the fire to the hollow, pulling her away from it.

At dusk, the coyote stretched and rose. Without so much

as a look back, he trotted from the camp and into the woods. "Jerk," Raymond muttered, watching him go.

There was no sign of the coyote the following morning, so Raymond ran as fast as he could to the spot in the woods where his fishing gear lay strewn across the earth. He gathered it up and raced back to the hollow. He found the small can of chicken and opened it. His mouth watered. He hadn't eaten in almost a whole day but he offered the entire thing to Rosie. After a few minutes of prodding, she finally ate it. Raymond sat beside her, eating another chocolate bar.

He brushed his teeth in the creek and splashed water on his face, shuddering from the cold. Bathing was out of the question. Rosie's licking had given way to gnawing. Raymond examined the wound. The entire top of her paw was licked clean of fur and it had a bright pink rawness to it that made Raymond recoil. The cut had grown in size and had started to ooze yellow pus that Raymond couldn't remove no matter how he tried to clean it. "Quit it, Rosie," he pleaded as she gnawed at the wound. He tried to make her lie back so he could rub her belly. But she just leaned up and kept on chewing.

At the children's home, there had been a boy who cut his foot on the rusty shower drain. He didn't tell anyone about it and tried to bandage the cut himself. Raymond remembered seeing the cut in the bathroom one morning. It looked like Rosie's did now. The boy had woken up a few nights later, screaming. An ambulance took him away and the children's home guardians never told them what happened to the boy. But they did have people come and replace all the shower drains.

Raymond slept uneasily that night and woke the next morning wet with sweat. He propped himself on his elbow. Rosie was burning up. Her paw was red and swollen and the yellow ooze was now a sickening green color. Raymond laid his head on his dog's chest. He didn't have a choice. He would have to try to find some help. He took a T-shirt from his duffel bag and ripped the sleeve, tying it around Rosie's paw. He dressed in his warmest clothes and carefully gathered her in his arms. He took a deep breath and began the long walk into town.

It was midmorning when they reached town and Raymond was exhausted. Eager to find help, he had kept moving in the woods, stopping only to readjust his grip on Rosie. Not a single car passed him on the country road that led to downtown. He stood at a cross street holding Rosie. The town seemed totally dead. He passed a gas station and a few fast-food restaurants, all closed. When he made it to the Shop-N-Save grocery store, there was a car in the parking lot but it appeared to be broken down, piled with snow that the sun had not yet melted away.

Raymond continued along the road, desperate to see someone, anyone who could offer help. He walked through the deserted town square, past the empty town hall and the closed shops. A car turned the corner. He tried to wave it down, still cradling Rosie in his arms, but it kept moving without slowing. He kept walking until he reached the edge of town where the shops stopped and the houses began. He stopped at a small house on the corner. He could see the TV inside and thought about what he would say if he knocked and someone came to the door. *Hello, I've been living in the woods and my dog is hurt. Can you help us?* He sighed and resolved that he had to at least try. He was just about to push through the small gate when a car pulled up behind him.

"Hey, kid," the driver said. It was the man from the river. Raymond recognized his white beard and old baseball hat. "What're you doing out here?"

"I . . . My dog is hurt. She needs help and everywhere is closed."

The man hesitated. Then he barked, "Get in." Raymond thought about all the lessons he had learned as a child about not getting into cars with strangers. Rosie licked his ear. He was out of options. Raymond pulled open the door to the back seat and lay Rosie down. Then he got in the front.

"Buckle your seat belt," the man said, his voice gruff and scratchy. Raymond buckled up. The car was clean despite its age and had the faint smell of rain and pipe tobacco. "What are you doing walking the streets?" the man asked. "Do your parents know you're out like this?" Raymond was prepared for the question.

"They're on vacation," he said. "We were going fishing

at the river and my dog got hurt." The man was silent for a moment, watching the road ahead of him.

"By the smell of it, that wound has been festering for at least a few days."

Raymond glanced back at Rosie, and fear crept over him. "My folks are away and I didn't know what to do. I tried to clean it but—"

"It's infected," the man cut in.

"Yeah, I guess so," said Raymond. "Can we take her somewhere?"

"Not today. Everything's closed for Christmas."

Raymond didn't say anything. He hadn't realized that it was Christmas Day. He thought of Rosie and looked ahead. He was grateful for the man's silence as he turned around and drove back into the country. He turned off the main road and onto a side street. Raymond recognized the road that he had just walked to town on and knew he had passed by there earlier that morning. They turned again and drove down a long dirt road until they reached a small cabin.

"Let's get her inside," the man said, taking the keys from the ignition. He climbed out of the car. Raymond did the same and the man was already halfway in the back, pulling Rosie gently out. He carried her up the small steps to the porch and Raymond followed. "Get the door," he ordered, and Raymond obeyed, following him into the warm cabin.

Like the car, the cabin was clean but had the feeling of being lived in. There was an old couch and an armchair in the living room arranged neatly around a woodburning fireplace. Off the living room was a small kitchen. The man shoved a newspaper from the kitchen table and laid Rosie down. Raymond watched as he removed the torn bit of T-shirt and inspected the wound. Without a word, he opened a cupboard and pulled out a few small bottles and a mesh bag. He laid them on the table next to Rosie.

"It'll take some doing," he said finally, "but I think we should be able to save the leg."

"Save the—" Raymond broke off, horrified. "You mean, she could lose her leg?"

"The leg is the least of her worries if we can't get this infection controlled. How long has she been running a fever?"

"Since this morning," Raymond choked out. "Please. Please help her."

The man grunted. "Hold her down," he said, directing Raymond to stand on the other side of the table. He filled a syringe and while Raymond pressed himself into his dog, the man pushed the liquid into her leg. Raymond could feel Rosie relax beneath him and he began to panic.

"Is she—" he cried.

"No. Just put out." The man began the busywork of cleaning and tending the wound. When he started to cut away at the rotting flesh, Raymond felt his stomach turn. "If you're going to be sick, do it in the bathroom down the hall." Raymond nodded and, clutching his stomach, ran from the room.

When he made it to the bathroom, he heaved a few times before slumping to the floor. He hadn't eaten and there wasn't anything in his stomach to throw up. It writhed and clenched in protest. Raymond took a few deep breaths and steadied himself. He stood and turned on the faucet at the sink, splashing water onto his face. Then he bent and took a few small sips.

He walked back down the hall slowly, his head reeling. He studied the framed pictures on the wall, trying to focus. There were a few of a young boy: a school picture, and one where he was older and in an army uniform. There was a picture of a young man who had to be the man from the river, standing in a boat with the boy, smiling and holding a huge fish. The house was quiet. At the end of the hall, there was a framed medal with a ribbon attached and under it an inscription that read: *The Medal of Honor awarded to Jacob Robert Castiglione.*

"You gonna hang around all day or are you gonna come and help me?" the man called from the kitchen, making Raymond jump.

"Sorry," Raymond said, walking back into the room. "What can I do?"

"Open that cupboard above the sink and get out the wooden box." Raymond did as he was told, bringing the small box to the table. The man opened it and Raymond watched as he riffled through the small instruments until he found what he was looking for.

"She'll make it," the man said. He glanced up at Raymond, who was still a bit shaky and green around the edges. "What's your name, kid?"

"Raymond. Raymond Hurley."

"Well, Raymond Hurley, I found you just in time. Any longer and we might be having a different talk entirely."

Raymond gripped the back of a chair for support. Then he sat down and stroked Rosie's fur. He couldn't lose Rosie. Not Rosie. "How do you know how to do this?" he asked.

The man was quiet for a few seconds and then said, "I was a surgeon once. Dogs aren't that different from humans. But you'll want to get her checked out by a vet all the same when we're done here."

"Yes sir," Raymond said.

"*Sir* is for soldiers and that hasn't been me for a long time. The name's Jacob, but you can call me Stigs." Stigs glanced up at Raymond and then back down at Rosie. "You look like you haven't slept in days, kid. There's an extra bedroom back there. Go on and rest. We're going to be here for a while."

Raymond looked at his sleeping dog. She looked so peaceful. Like she might just be napping instead of undergoing kitchen surgery. Stigs was right, Raymond hadn't slept well in days. He hesitated, not wanting to leave Rosie and not sure if he should trust this man. Experience told him most people could not be trusted. But there was something about this house, about Stigs, and the gentle way he handled Rosie, that felt comforting to Raymond. He could already feel himself relax a little just being there, despite Rosie's condition.

"Go on," Stigs encouraged. "She'll be okay. I'll wake you if she needs you."

Raymond nodded. He found the spare bedroom easily enough. It was a small cabin and there weren't many rooms.

He looked longingly at the double bed but wondered how he would be able to rest with Rosie out there, sick. But as soon as his head hit the pillow, he fell asleep.

When he woke up, it took him a minute to remember where he was. Thinking of Rosie, he shot up in bed and instantly regretted it. His stomach was tender from retching and hunger and his head spun. He swung his feet to the floor and steadied himself before pushing off the bed and going to find Rosie. A fire was burning in the living room and the kitchen was empty. Raymond panicked, looking for any sign of his dog. Stigs came through the front door carrying an armful of wood.

"Where is she?" Raymond half screamed.

"She's just there at the end of the couch," Stigs said calmly. Rosie lay on the square cushion. She didn't raise her head but her tail wagged at the sound of Raymond's voice. Her fur was the same color as the couch and he hadn't noticed her lying there.

"Hey, girl," he said as he knelt beside her. "You're all right now. " He stroked her fur.

"Had to give her a little something for the pain. She got sick when she woke up. She'll be a little out of it for a few hours." Only then did Raymond notice that it was dark.

"How long was I sleeping?" he asked.

"Long time," said Stigs. "All day."

Raymond didn't know what to say. "I guess we will get out of your hair. Thank you, sir."

Stigs flinched at the word *sir* and shook his head. "It's Stigs," he said. "You can't move that dog tonight. Maybe not even tomorrow. I've got a phone if you need to call your folks but you better just leave her with me for now."

"Oh," said Raymond. "Okay." He made no move to get the phone.

Stigs looked at Raymond. "So, your folks are out of town, you said?"

Raymond nodded.

"Any chance they'll be back before tomorrow?"

Raymond shook his head.

"Right. Well, I guess they won't miss you then if you stay here tonight. Dinner's almost ready, anyhow."

Raymond's stomach groaned in response. It had been days since he had eaten properly.

"Help me set the table," Stigs said.

Raymond helped Stigs set out the plates and utensils. Stigs served him a large portion of beef stew. Raymond was already shoveling it in his mouth before Stigs sat down.

"Good lord, boy. When's the last time you ate?"

"Sorry," Raymond muttered with his mouth full. He tried to slow down. The stew had big chunks of tender meat and soft potatoes and Raymond thought it tasted like heaven itself. He ate three servings and half a loaf of bread before setting his spoon down. He looked over at Rosie, who was still sleeping on the couch.

"Better not give her anything heavy tonight," said Stigs, still eating his meal. "But you can offer her a little broth if she'll take it."

Raymond spooned some of the liquid into his bowl and walked it over to Rosie. She raised her head and sniffed. Raymond rubbed her ears and she lapped up the broth and licked his hand before lying back down. Raymond's eyes watered. He had almost lost her. He gathered himself and stood, carrying the bowl back to the kitchen to set it in the sink.

"Tell me, Raymond," Stigs said, taking another bite. "What kind of kid doesn't know it's Christmas Day?"

Raymond tensed. He knew he had to be careful how he answered. What could he say? The kind of kid whose parents left him. The kind of kid who lives in a tree hollow in the woods. The kind of kid who has more important things to worry about than some dumb holiday. "Must've just slipped my mind."

Stigs didn't look convinced. But he didn't push the topic. "You're not from around here, are you?"

"No sir," said Raymond, and the old man flinched again.

"Call me Stigs," he said. "I didn't think so. I've lived here most of my life and know pretty much everybody around here there is to know. Which isn't saying much."

"We—my folks and I—we move around a lot. I just started at River Mill Middle this year." Stigs nodded and his eyebrows creased like he was remembering something he would rather not. "You live here alone?" Raymond asked, trying to change the subject.

Stigs nodded. "Have for a while now."

"The boy in the pictures, is he your son?" Raymond asked.

Stigs set his spoon down. "He was, yes."

"Oh." Raymond wished he hadn't asked. "I'm sorry." Stigs stood and began clearing the table. "Here," said Raymond, grabbing the stew pot. "Let me." It was the least he could do.

Stigs grunted and walked out of the kitchen, leaving Raymond to clean the dishes and put away the leftovers. Stigs prodded the fire and added a few logs. Then he sat on the couch next to Rosie and stroked her fur.

When Raymond was finished in the kitchen, he joined him, sitting down in the armchair. He relished the warmth of the fire. He was thankful that he didn't have to go back to the woods, at least for tonight. It was silent for a long time as they watched the flames lick the inside of the fireplace.

Finally, Stigs got up. "I'll move her into the spare room so she can sleep with you if you'd like."

"I can carry her," Raymond offered but Stigs was already lifting Rosie gently from the couch. Raymond followed them down the hall. Stigs gently laid Rosie at the foot of the spare bed. "If she wakes in the night and gets sick, just holler for me."

Raymond nodded. "Thank you," he said. Stigs just grunted and shut the door behind him, leaving Raymond and Rosie alone in the small room. Rosie's tail was wagging. She was more alert than before, and Raymond gently moved her to the top of the bed and crawled in beside her, careful not to jostle her bandaged leg.

Raymond lay awake into the night, petting Rosie and

wondering how he'd got there. He studied the pictures on the walls of the small room and the cracks in the ceiling. Stigs seemed like a nice man, but could he really trust him? He had the urge to get up and leave right then, go back to the hollow. He propped himself up and Rosie licked his arm. Raymond remembered that he couldn't move her.

The first Christmas that Raymond could remember was the one when he was six. His parents had been invited on some ski trip and hadn't brought him. He had woken up on Christmas morning after two days alone. He had eaten all of the bologna and cheese that his parents had left him in the days prior and he was hungry.

He filled a pot with water, pushed a chair to the stove, and cooked a packet of ramen noodles. He didn't know to wait for the water to boil, and had dumped the contents in and waited. He remembered burning his tongue on the first bite and then not being able to taste the rest. It was the first meal he'd ever cooked for himself.

Raymond tried to relax now. He laid his head on the pillow. Rosie was already asleep again, softly snoring. "I guess you trust Stigs, huh?" whispered Raymond. When she didn't answer, he added, "Merry Christmas, Rosie," and lay awake, staring at the ceiling.

Chapter Thirteen

When Stigs inspected Rosie's leg the next day, he said she wasn't well enough to travel. Raymond still wasn't sure about the man but he also knew he didn't want to leave yet. He'd finally fallen asleep late last night and he'd woken up feeling like a whole new person. He felt rested. He wasn't starving. His back didn't ache. So he lied and told Stigs that his parents wouldn't be home until after the New Year. "They're going to a party and kids aren't allowed." It wasn't the truth but it wasn't exactly a lie either. If Raymond knew his parents, they probably would be at some party. And none of the parties his parents attended ever allowed kids.

Stigs poured a cup of coffee and sat down at the kitchen table. "Won't they be worried if they call home and don't get an answer?" he asked.

"We don't have a phone," Raymond said truthfully. "So even if they wanted to call, they couldn't."

Stigs looked at Raymond for a long time without responding. His eyebrows were pinched together in concentration. He took a sip of his coffee. Raymond wasn't sure if he should say something and he felt the urge again to just grab Rosie and run.

"All right, then," Stigs finally said, snapping Raymond out of it. "You'll stay for now. Until your parents are back."

Raymond let a breath out that he hadn't realized he was holding. "Besides," he continued. "I could use the help around here. These old bones aren't what they used to be." When Raymond didn't say anything, Stigs got up and walked to the door. As far as Raymond could tell, Stigs could get around just fine. He pulled on his coat and followed Stigs out the door.

Behind the cabin was a small building that Raymond hadn't noticed the day before. Stigs opened a little gate. "Come on, girls," he called, and Raymond watched as at least ten chickens came skirting out of their coop and through the gate. Raymond stood aside, letting them run past.

"Will they come back?" he asked. One of the hens was already past the car in the front drive.

"They will if they want to eat and stay warm," Stigs said. He tossed Raymond a basket, which he caught against his chest. "Grab the eggs, will ya? And be careful. Missy likes to lay hers on the ground."

Raymond grinned, wondering which of the chickens was Missy. Stigs cleaned the water bowls and raked out the mulch beneath the coop. Raymond finished collecting the eggs, which he found oddly satisfying.

"Grab that bucket up top there and feed them," Stigs said, pointing to the rafters.

Raymond did as he was told. He removed the lid with a pop. As soon as the chickens heard the sound, they were running from all directions back to the coop. Raymond stood quickly, momentarily stunned at the onrush of birds.

Stigs chuckled. "You better give them their treat before

they get angry." The chickens were already jumping and cackling at Raymond's feet. He grabbed a handful of the dried grubs and sprinkled them around. The birds happily accepted his offering, flapping their wings. Raymond tossed a few more handfuls. He laughed as the birds fought one another for one grub, when there were tons more right beside them.

Stigs turned the lights off under the water bowls and hung the rake back up on the wall. "We'll make sure they're closed back in the pen before dark," he said, leaving the gate open as he walked around the side of the house. Stigs dropped the eggs off inside and met Raymond out front.

They spent the rest of the morning dragging tree limbs and chopping them into firewood. They were splitting a large fallen tree up the hill from the cabin when Raymond spotted a familiar tree from the river.

"Hey, a paper tree," he said.

Stigs looked over his shoulder. "That is a river birch," he said. "They're pretty common in River Mill. Makes a good landscape tree."

"The bark makes a pretty good fire too," said Raymond, and immediately wished he hadn't. Stigs didn't seem to be bothered by the statement, though. He grunted and kept on working.

Stigs knew the name of every tree and plant in the surrounding woods. Raymond found himself pointing to trees, asking Stigs to name them. Most of the time he named them outright, other times he told Raymond to get back to work.

Stigs didn't talk much but Raymond didn't mind. He had

never been much of a talker anyway and it was nice to have somebody to just be quiet with for a while. He wondered what would happen if Harlin ever met Stigs. The thought made Raymond laugh out loud as he felled a small pine.

After they cleared and dragged the backwoods, they spent the rest of the afternoon fixing a busted water pipe around the side of the cabin. There was still a pile of wood to chop, but Stigs said it could wait until tomorrow.

That night, after the chickens were called back to their coop for the evening, Raymond helped Stigs batter fish fillets to fry. He thought about what a luxury a frying pan was. Stigs rolled sweet potatoes in tinfoil and popped them in the oven. He pulled field peas from the freezer and cooked them slowly on the stove. When the sweet potatoes were finished, he and Raymond sliced them open, adding pats of butter and spoonfuls of brown sugar. Raymond watched the butter and sugar melt into the potato and his mouth watered.

"You sure can eat," Stigs said, eyeing Raymond as he helped himself to seconds and thirds.

"Sorry," Raymond said, swallowing a mouthful.

"Been a while since I've had anyone to cook for. And anyway, the freezer's been needing a cleaning out." Raymond nodded and offered Rosie the leftover portion of his third fillet of fish. She ate it in one bite and Stigs grunted, smiling.

Raymond thought that this must be what families did. They

sat around the table making small talk about the meal or their day or laughing at the family pet while they ate spaghetti. He thought about his failed Thanksgiving dinner. Stigs made this feel so easy. Raymond's family had only ever successfully eaten a meal together once. *Once.* He took another bite of his peas.

"You said you moved here this year?" Stigs asked.

Raymond could hear the questioning tone and quietly begged himself to remain calm. He nodded.

"And your parents? They leave you like this often?" Raymond wanted to trust Stigs, but he knew that he had to be careful how he answered.

"Sometimes," Raymond replied, and took another bite of his sweet potato. He tried to appear unbothered by the questions.

Stigs was quiet for what felt like a long time. "You have any other family?"

Raymond shook his head. He thought Stigs would keep asking him questions, but the man just gave a final grunt and got up from the table. He dropped his plate in the sink and began washing the dishes.

Raymond joined him. When they were finished with the dishes, Stigs walked into the living room and didn't say another word for the rest of the night.

The next day, Raymond woke up early and took a long shower. He stood in the water until his fingers were wrinkled and his skin was red from the heat. He couldn't remember the last time he'd had a proper hot shower. He would've stayed there longer but Stigs came to the door and barked, "Hey! Leave some hot water for the rest of us, will ya?" Raymond quickly turned the water off and scrambled out of the bathroom.

That afternoon, he helped Stigs patch a hole in the roof of the chicken coop, and they chopped the rest of the fallen tree in the afternoon. Stigs fried eggs and sausage, and they sat on the porch drinking hot cocoa after dinner. Snow still clung to the ground, but it was a nice night for being outside.

Raymond had saved a piece of soft wood from the chopping block and was using one of Stigs's steak knives to whittle it.

"Who taught you how to do that?" Stigs asked.

"Nobody." Raymond shrugged. "Just taught myself."

"Hand it here," said Stigs. "I want to try."

Stigs's hands weren't as steady as Raymond's, and he kept taking out big chunks of wood and cussing.

"You have to hold your thumb out," said Raymond. He couldn't help but laugh, which would elicit glares from Stigs and more cussing.

"I thought you said you were a surgeon?" Raymond joked.

"Yeah, that's what I said." Stigs took a large chunk out of the wood by mistake and groaned. He handed the knife and the wood back to Raymond. "What about it?"

Raymond thought for a moment. "Don't surgeons make a lot of money?"

Stigs chuckled, and Raymond immediately apologized. He wasn't trying to be rude. He loved the little cabin but couldn't help but notice that it wasn't exactly the fanciest place to live. It had one bathroom and two small bedrooms just big enough for beds. It wasn't wired for heat like most houses were. It relied solely on the woodburning fireplace, and the bedrooms got cold at night. Stigs seemed to be constantly making repairs and fixing things that were broken. And although they were clean, the furnishings were old and tattered.

"Some do, I suppose. But I was an army surgeon and army surgeons make the same as any other officer."

"Oh," said Raymond, smoothing out the edges of the wood with the knife.

"I didn't have much taste for surgery after I got back," said Stigs. He took a sip of his coffee. "Or anything else for that matter."

Raymond nodded. "Except fishing," he said. "You still like to fish."

"Yeah, I still like to fish. Fish don't talk and the river never asked me for anything in return." He stood up. "It's getting cold out here. Come on in when you're done." And he was through the door before Raymond could ask him any more questions.

Raymond sat outside whittling the wood for another hour. He thought about what Stigs had said. Raymond had been fishing for so long and he'd never stopped to wonder why he loved it so much. Now that he thought about it, every time he needed to get away from his parents, or just be alone, he had gone fishing. It was quiet and peaceful. He could rely on fishing for that and Raymond could never rely on much else. Except for Rosie. And maybe Harlin.

When he was finished, he walked inside and set the small wooden fish he'd carved on the kitchen table before carefully scooping Rosie from the couch and going to bed.

Raymond did what he could to help out around the cabin, cleaning up after meals and chopping wood into the evening. Stigs kept a fire going in the house all the time so at least the living room was always warm. By the fourth day, the wood-pile on the front porch was stacked nearly to the ceiling. Rosie started to hobble around on her three good legs, and Raymond helped Stigs inspect and clean the wound, careful to follow directions.

Raymond had never met anyone like Stigs. Despite his crankiness and his sometimes gruff responses, he liked the old man. They seemed to understand each other without speaking. On the fourth night of Raymond's stay, it snowed again and Raymond helped Stigs shovel the steps and dig out the car the next day. Then they wrapped the car tires in chains. There was a small slab of concrete at the bottom of the front steps and Raymond scraped the shovel across it. In the corner, there were three sets of handprints pressed into the concrete, two adults' and one child's. Raymond resisted the urge to bend over and place his own hands on the child's handprints.

"Did you live here when you were a kid?" he asked Stigs, who was replacing the light bulb in the fixture on the front porch.

"Not exactly," Stigs said. "It was my family's hunting cabin. I used to come here with my father sometimes. It's about the only good memory I have of the man." He screwed in the light bulb and crawled down from the ladder to get the fixture. Raymond nodded. He didn't want to pry but he had so many questions. He wanted to know more about Stigs. About his family. He couldn't help himself.

"Was your family from here, then?" Raymond asked.

Stigs held the fixture in place and began screwing it back to the porch ceiling. "My father was, yes. My mother was from somewhere on the West Coast, I think. She died when I was just a baby. My father never said much about her." Raymond stopped shoveling and looked up at Stigs.

Stigs climbed down from the ladder, reached inside the door, and flipped the switch. The light blinked on. "There," he said. Rosie whined at his feet so he bent over and gave her a pat. Raymond started shoveling again and Stigs sat on the top porch step, petting Rosie.

Stigs continued this time without being asked. "I grew up about fifteen miles from here at an orphanage off the highway a little past Hillsborough." He said it so matter-of-factly that Raymond was taken aback though he tried not to show it. He dragged the shovel across the slab until he met gravel. "I guess they don't really call them orphanages anymore," Stigs continued. "It's a school now, I'm told. River Mill was the only town with a middle school back then, so we all got bused over. And my father used to come pick me up a few times a year and bring me over here to hunt. My old man wasn't much of a father and he knew it."

Stigs took a breath. "From what I can tell, neither is yours. But we make do with what we're given, don't we? That doesn't make it right but it is what it is." Raymond didn't respond so Stigs continued. "I was sixteen when my father died and I left the orphanage and moved in here."

"Alone?" Raymond asked.

It took Stigs a moment to answer, and Raymond thought he could see the shadow of a smile on his face. "Not always," Stigs said. "But there are worse things than being alone, Raymond." Raymond looked back down at the shovel. Stigs stood and went inside. Rosie followed.

At the children's home, parents were allowed to visit on Saturdays only. One little girl who was about Raymond's age used to sit on the bench outside of the visitation lounge and wait for her mother every Saturday. When her mother showed up, she would complain the entire time about what a burden it was to be visiting. Raymond remembered overhearing her the first few weekends that he was there. The girl's mother never made an effort to keep her voice down, and the whole visitation room could hear. It was always about how lucky the girl was that she had a mother who showed up, and couldn't they do something about the air-conditioning, or couldn't visitation be on a more convenient day? At least Raymond's parents had seemed to be trying at the time. After a while, Raymond had a hard time looking at the girl when his own parents showed up, so he would just look at her shoes when they passed by. She always wore Converse tennis shoes with red laces.

There are worse things than being alone, Raymond agreed with Stigs. He finished shoveling the drive and then chopped the rest of the wood before going back inside.

By the end of the week, Rosie was getting around much better and was able to go up and down the porch steps on her own. She was eating more and Raymond knew that their time at the cabin was coming to a close. On the morning of New Year's Eve, Raymond woke up early to make breakfast. He gathered eggs from the hens and scrambled them. He did his best with the bacon, only burning it a little. He and Stigs sat at the table and ate without speaking. When breakfast was done, Stigs took his plate to the sink and walked to the front door.

"Come on, then," he said. "There's work to be done." Raymond grabbed his coat. After they tended the chickens, Stigs pulled an old broken space heater out of the shed. "Probably just needs a good cleaning," he said, but Raymond wasn't so sure. It looked ancient. The bolts and screws were rusted together.

Stigs noticed the expression on Raymond's face. "She's got at least as much life left in her as I do." Raymond made another face and Stigs scowled. "Watch it." Raymond smiled and grabbed a wrench from the toolbox.

By the end of the day, the space heater was cleaned up with

new bolts and running like a dream. Raymond helped Stigs carry it into the cabin and they plugged it in, in Raymond's room.

That night as Raymond lay in bed, he thought about how his winter break had turned out very different from how he thought it would. He had told Stigs that his parents would be home after the New Year so he knew he would have to leave the next day. He thought about Stigs cooking him dinners and showing him how to do things, helping him learn the right way to chop wood and fixing the space heater so Raymond wouldn't get cold. His parents had never done anything with Raymond. They couldn't even be bothered to stick around for Christmas or at least say goodbye.

He sat up, jolting Rosie awake beside him. He threw the blanket off and got out of bed. He felt like his chest, his throat, his heart, was going to explode. He wanted to scream and hit something. He wanted to run. He pulled his shoes on and walked quickly down the hall and out the door. He practically leaped off the front porch and ran into the darkness until the gravel turned to dirt beneath his feet. When he finally came to a stop, his face wet with tears, he screamed as if his parents were standing right there in front of him. The sound poured out of him and wrapped around him in frozen clouds. Wherever his parents were right now, they wouldn't hear him. Even if they were standing right in front of Raymond, they wouldn't hear him. He stood there in the darkness, swallowing air and panting until his breath became steady. He wiped his face, turned around, and walked slowly back to the cabin.

Stigs was standing on the porch in his coat and shoes, holding a flashlight when Raymond appeared. Raymond knew he should apologize but was suddenly unable to use his voice. Stigs held the door open for him without saying a word.

The next morning, Raymond found Stigs in the kitchen drinking a cup of coffee.

"Your folks'll be coming home today, then." It was more of a statement than a question. Raymond couldn't bring himself to say anything so he just nodded.

"Listen, kid, is there anything I can do to help? Someone I could call for you?"

"No," Raymond said, a little too quickly. He'd heard this question before. He corrected himself and tried to shrug it off. "No, really. I'm fine."

Stigs studied Raymond. "What about Rosie? You think you'll be able to get her to a vet?" Raymond didn't answer. "No, I didn't think so. Well, her leg is healed anyhow. I'd feel better if she was properly looked at by someone, but I think she'll be okay. She's a tough ol' girl." Rosie had come into the room and affectionately rubbed her back against Stigs. He patted her head. Over the past week, Rosie had become very attached to the old man, following him from room to room.

Stigs took a deep breath. "When you're ready, I'll get you home."

"That's okay," said Raymond, standing quickly. "We can walk from here. It's not too far and I can carry Rosie if she has trouble."

Stigs didn't respond right away. He was staring out the kitchen window, his back to Raymond.

"My son was like you," he said finally. "He talked more than you and was always more eager than he needed to be. But he was smart. And he managed a lot on his own. More than he should've."

"What happened to him?" Every time Stigs had mentioned his son, which wasn't often, he used the past tense.

"Afghanistan," Stigs said, still looking out the window. He hung his head for a minute and then turned around to face Raymond. "One way or another, war takes your life. Whether you come back or not. Whether you keep on living or not. It changes you and you can't ever get back to who you were before. No matter how hard you try."

Raymond looked at his friend. He thought about the picture of the younger Stigs smiling with his son in the boat. He wondered if Stigs was talking about his son or himself. He guessed maybe both.

After breakfast, Raymond made his bed and picked up around the spare room. Stigs handed him a grocery bag of a few wrapped-up leftovers, some protein bars, and medicine for Rosie. He also dropped in the few cans of dog food that he had left. He gave him instructions on how to administer the medicine, and Raymond nodded, listening carefully. He handed Stigs the old fur army hat that he had let him borrow, but Stigs shook his head. "Keep it," he said. He gestured to Rosie. "If she needs anything, just bring her by the house."

Raymond nodded again. He wanted to hug the old man but couldn't imagine actually doing it. "Thank you," he said instead, holding out his hand. Stigs grunted, shaking it.

Then Raymond tried to let go, but Stigs held it firm. "Whatever it is, kid, you can tell me when you're ready. Maybe I can help."

Raymond did want to tell him. He wanted to tell him everything. Stigs would understand, wouldn't he? Stigs would help him. Raymond opened his mouth. And then he thought of every other time in his life when he had asked for help, every other time when he had tried to rely on someone else. He thought of his parents and of the children's home. He thought of the social worker's car driving away down his street. He thought of the blue duffel bag sitting open on the front step of the trailer. No. Stigs was his friend, a great friend. But he couldn't help Raymond.

Raymond closed his mouth and gave a final nod, letting go of the old man's hand. He made his way down the front steps with Rosie hopping down behind him.

"I don't go fishing much in the winter," Stigs called from the porch. "But when I do, I usually go on Saturdays."

Raymond turned toward his friend. "Maybe I'll see you there then." But Stigs had already gone back inside the cabin and was closing the door behind him.

Chapter Fourteen

Raymond's camp wasn't all that far from the cabin. He and Rosie crossed the bridge on the road that went over the river and they made their way back through the trees. Raymond's muscles tensed against the cold. He had grown used to the warmth of the cabin. Rosie didn't fall behind much but Raymond carried her for the last little bit anyway.

Snow covered the ground, and Raymond had to stop a few times to remember which way to go. When he found the creek, he easily made his way back to the camp. When he was almost there, the thought occurred to him that he had been gone from the camp for a week. He wondered if his food and belongings would still be there, or if animals had carried them off in his absence.

They were almost there when Rosie tensed. Raymond set her down, looking at the fresh paw prints through the snow. Rosie sniffed the earth, pacing back and forth, trying to pick up the scent. The coyote peered out from the hollowed tree. Raymond had almost forgotten about the animal. Rosie growled. Raymond looked at the coyote, who was lying on his sleeping bag. His brow furrowed. Coyotes weren't necessarily territorial but he might get aggressive if he thought it was his home now.

The coyote jumped lazily from the tree. He stretched

his forelegs in front of him, arched his back, and yawned. Still stretched forward, his tail began to wag. Rosie snorted. Raymond walked slowly toward the animal with his arms stretched wide. He let the coyote sniff the back of his hand. His tail wagged again and he lunged forward, trying to nudge Rosie in the ribs. She snapped her teeth at him. The coyote was unbothered. He stood and trotted past Raymond, brushing his legs with his tail. Raymond watched him disappear into the woods.

"I think he's sorry," Raymond told Rosie. Rosie huffed and then whimpered. Raymond knew she was thinking about Stigs. "I know you miss him, girl. We'll see him again soon." Raymond missed the old man too. And the cabin. He sighed and began to clean up around the camp.

The coyote, or some other animal, had eaten all the candy bars and packaged food, leaving wrappers lying around in the snow. The only thing left was a small tin of pears. Raymond pulled the sleeping bag from the hollow. He shook it and hung it over the roots to air out. Then he swept out the inside of the tree with his hands. He set his scattered wood carvings back upright, running his fingers along their curves. He unpacked the leftover sandwiches from the bag he carried and tucked them in the back. Something heavy was still in the bag. He reached in and pulled out a Swiss Army knife. Stigs must've put it in there for Raymond. He flicked open the blade and smiled. It was used but in great condition. He slipped the knife into his pocket and climbed out of the tree.

It had been almost two weeks since the Winter Jamboree

but it felt like so much longer. He picked up the trash around the camp and used it to build a small fire. He pulled a box of matches from his coat pocket and hoped Stigs wouldn't notice (or mind) that they'd gone missing. He would have to find more wood for his stores tomorrow. He thought of the stack of firewood on Stigs's front porch and wished he had an axe or even a hatchet. He wiped the snow from a log and sat down.

School would be starting the day after tomorrow, and Raymond hadn't even thought about his homework. Ms. Marcus had assigned an essay on *The Outsiders*. They were supposed to write what the theme of the book was and use examples as evidence. Ms. Marcus had already questioned him about his slipping grades and he didn't want to give her any more cause for concern. But he didn't feel much like writing today. Plus, he also had about four pages of a math review that he hadn't even looked at.

He pulled the math book from his book bag and thumbed through it. For the rest of the day, Raymond did his math homework by the fire, throwing in sticks when needed. When night fell, he ate a sandwich and opened a can of dog food for Rosie. Then he crawled into the sleeping bag next to his dog and tried to get comfortable. It was a far cry from the double bed he'd slept in all week. A coyote howled in the distance and Rosie groaned in response. Raymond laughed.

As he lay in the cold hollow, he couldn't help but think about Stigs and the past week. He thought about Stigs's life and wondered what he had been like as a father. Despite himself, he thought about his own parents again. He wondered if they really had gone to a New Year's party somewhere and if they ever thought about him. He wondered if he would ever see them again. He kept on wondering until he fell asleep.

The next morning, the coyote was standing outside the hollow, tail wagging, with a freshly caught rabbit hanging limply from his mouth. It looked like he had chewed one leg almost clean off. He set the rabbit down in the snow and looked up eagerly. Rosie huffed and laid her head back down.

"Is that for us?" Raymond asked, rubbing the sleep from his eyes. The coyote nudged the rabbit forward in response.

Raymond pulled his shoes on. He hopped out of the tree and the coyote hopped too, copying him. Raymond laughed. "You're just a big puppy, aren't you?" The coyote wagged his tail.

Raymond picked up the rabbit. "I guess this is as good a breakfast as any," he said to the coyote and went about the business of trying to skin the animal.

Skinning and preparing the rabbit was a little easier than the squirrel had been and the sharp Swiss Army knife made a big difference. Raymond laid the rabbit fur on a log to dry out. He built a fire and sharpened a new roasting stick, unable to find the old one. He'd had a week of home-cooked meals from Stigs's kitchen, and feeling inspired, he decided he would become more efficient.

He gathered up as many sticks as he could find and made

a pile by his fire. He built an A-frame of sticks that he wedged into the ground on either side of the firepit. There were grooves on either side so Raymond could set the skewered rabbit between them to roast. He monitored the arrangement, turning the animal every few minutes. It was an effective system, but it did require Raymond's full attention. When the rabbit was cooked, he took a leg to the hollow, laying it down for Rosie. She huffed and turned in the other direction.

"You have to eat, Rosie. Doctor's orders." She didn't move. Raymond ate his fill and tossed the rest of the rabbit to the coyote, who ripped it apart unceremoniously. Rosie watched him from the hollow and finally gave in, pulling little pieces of the meat from the bone, showing the coyote how an animal *should* eat.

Raymond smiled. He wrapped her medicine in a piece of skin, and Rosie ate it without protest. "Good girl," he said, and she licked his hand.

Raymond spent the day collecting sticks to lay in the sun to dry, carving wood with his new knife, and doing his homework. The coyote bounced around the camp, tossing snow in the air with his nose and trying his hardest to get Rosie to play. She was trying her best to ignore the animal, but he wasn't getting the message. When she snapped at him, it only made him more excited. Finally, he gave up, running circles around the camp and rolling in the snow. He would fall asleep and then just as suddenly wake up and begin running again. Raymond watched him, laughing, and tried to focus on his essay for Ms. Marcus.

He finished around nightfall. It wasn't his best work but it would have to do. He ate the tin of pears. He packed his book bag and shook out his clothes for the next day. He sniffed a dingy T-shirt. He really needed to clean them again. Stigs had washed and dried Raymond's hoodie and jeans, loaning him some clothes one evening. Raymond thought that he could at least wear those tomorrow and he would wash the others after school. He walked to the creek and brushed his teeth. He was relieved to find that despite the cold, the creek had not yet frozen over. Then, not bothering to stamp out the dimming fire, he crawled into the hollow. Rosie jumped up behind him and growled at the coyote, who stood at the opening. It looked for a minute like the coyote was going to jump in after them but he yawned and lay down at the base of the tree outside.

"Hank," Raymond said, and the coyote looked up. "We'll call you Hank."

Chapter Fifteen

Raymond was up before the sun rose the next morning and had already dressed for school and brushed his teeth when Hank stretched and sauntered out of the camp. Raymond gave Rosie the last of her medicine and rechecked that he had everything in his book bag. He didn't know why, but he felt nervous to return to school. Nothing had really changed, but he felt exposed somehow, in danger of being found out. He still didn't know who had given him the five dollars and the thought made him anxious all over again. He walked the tree line to the bus lot early and watched as teachers parked and let themselves into the building. When the first bus pulled in, Raymond waited until everyone had unloaded and the bus was pulling out before he stepped out of the woods and followed the crowd into the cafeteria.

He was almost finished eating his eggs and had already tucked the biscuit away for Rosie when Harlin joined him. He was wearing a brand-new racing T-shirt and was grinning from ear to ear. "Hey, Ray!"

"Hey, Harlin." Raymond smiled. He couldn't help but admit to himself that he had missed Harlin over the break.

"Did you have a good Christmas? I sure did. My gran pulled out all the stops. I wasn't sure if she would on account of still being pretty mad at me about getting suspended. But she sure surprised me. Cooked up a big dinner with ham, corn bread, gravy . . ." Harlin closed his eyes, remembering the meal.

"That sounds really nice, Harlin," Raymond said.

"Sure was." Then he lowered his voice a bit and said, "We drove out to see my mom too. She was happy to see us. Said she might be gettin' out by next Christmas, ahead of schedule and everything."

"That's great," Raymond said, and he was genuinely happy for his friend. He wanted to tell Harlin about Rosie getting hurt and Stigs and even Hank, but he knew he couldn't. What Raymond had thought would be the worst Christmas of his life had turned out to be the best one. So instead, he asked Harlin questions about his break and let Harlin recount each day, taking breaths between mouthfuls of eggs and grits.

They began learning about ecosystems in science and Raymond really enjoyed listening to Mr. Rosen's talk. "There are all kinds of wild animals that live right here in our backyard. But we rarely see them. Why is that?"

"Because we don't live in the woods," Joseph Banker called out, and everyone laughed. Raymond looked down at the table, trying to become invisible.

"Yes," said Mr. Rosen. "Partly. But we don't see them because they don't want to be seen. We aren't part of their ecosystem so we might pass right by them without even noticing. If you see an animal like a coyote or a bobcat around here, it's usually because they *want* you to see them." Mr. Rosen explained that coyotes were apex predators but they were also scavengers, which makes them very adaptable. "In some areas, coyote populations have been greatly diminished by killing and trapping. Humans sometimes think coyotes are bad but really they are just playing their part and doing what comes naturally. Things only get messed up when we start interfering."

Raymond couldn't help but think about Hank. Raymond wondered if there were other coyotes in the woods that he couldn't see. He wondered if they saw him. The thought made him shudder.

Lexi looked over. "You cold?" she asked.

"What? Oh, no. I'm okay," said Raymond. Mr. Rosen asked the class to read the chapter on ecosystems and take notes. Raymond worked quietly, wondering what Hank and Rosie were up to.

In English class, Ms. Marcus had everyone write a New Year's resolution instead of answering the question of the day. Raymond wrote that his resolution was to spend more time fishing with his new friend, Stigs. Ms. Marcus walked around the room making comments about each resolution. When she read Raymond's, her smile turned down and she stared at Raymond. She opened her mouth to say something but then closed it again and moved to the next person. Raymond looked at his paper. Maybe Ms. Marcus didn't like fishing, he thought. She collected the theme essays and gave them a news article to read about New Year's traditions.

The rest of the day went on without incident. They had

endurance training in gym, and by the time Raymond made it to art, he was drenched in sweat. The nervous feeling Raymond had that morning abated as the day went on, and disappeared entirely while he listened to Harlin prattle on in art.

"Did you know that a coyote is an apex specimen?" Harlin asked. They were sketching portraits of each other and Harlin and Raymond were partners. Raymond was finding it difficult to sketch someone who wouldn't stop moving.

"That means," Harlin went on, "that they are *very* important to their ecosystem. Without them, everything gets all messed up."

"I think it's apex *predator*," Raymond said, trying to concentrate. "Stop moving, will you?"

After class, Raymond waited with Harlin until his bus came. He pulled a small wooden car that he had carved out of his book bag and handed it to Harlin. "Happy birthday," he said. "I didn't know exactly what day it was but you said it was in January."

Harlin held the small car with both hands, quietly turning it over.

"It isn't much," said Raymond, feeling embarrassed.

"It's great," Harlin said, and for one horrifying second, Raymond thought Harlin was going to cry. Then he cleared his throat and added, "Thanks, man."

Raymond smiled. The bus pulled in and the door swung open for kids to climb on. "See you tomorrow," Raymond said.

"See ya tomorrow, buddy!" Harlin called, and climbed into

the bus. Raymond slipped into the woods as the bus drove away.

The next day, Mr. Rosen reminded the students about the approaching science fair. The class had started talking about the scientific process before the break and they would be putting their efforts to work. Raymond groaned. He had forgotten all about the project. "You may work in pairs, or on your own. The choice is yours. I will need you to submit your ideas to me by the end of the week."

Raymond thumbed through one of the manuals on his desk, wondering what he would be able to complete in just a few short weeks. Mr. Rosen was supplying the science boards and was giving them some time in class, but most of the work would need to be completed outside of the classroom.

"Do you have a partner yet?" Lexi asked. After a few seconds with no response, she tried again: "Raymond? Do you have a partner yet?" Raymond hadn't realized that she was talking to him.

"Me?" he said. "No. Why? Do you want to be my partner?" He had figured he would be working alone, as he usually did.

Lexi smiled. "Sure! I mean, only if you want to. You are way better at science than I am so I probably wouldn't be the best choice."

"No," Raymond said. "I mean, yes! I'll be your partner,"

he added quickly. "Do you have any ideas? I haven't really thought about it much."

"Just one, but it might be silly. My dad's a dentist and I was thinking about doing something with teeth."

"I love teeth!" Raymond said. And then realizing that *I love teeth* probably wasn't something that normal people say, he said, "I mean, that's a great idea. What were you thinking?" He shook his head. *Get it together, Raymond*, he thought.

Lexi giggled. "I don't know exactly, but my dad's always talking about how bad people's teeth can get. He pulls so many that are rotten or decayed. He practically outlawed sweets and sodas at our house because he says they ruin your smile. I've seen a few of the teeth that he's pulled. It's pretty gross, actually."

"He keeps them? The teeth?"

"Only the really decayed ones. I think he wants to scare me into taking care of mine."

"Well, you obviously take care of yours," said Raymond, and he felt his cheeks grow warm.

The two spent the rest of the period talking about the different experiments they might do. They turned in their proposal at the end of class and made a plan to meet in the library the next day to get the rest of the project planned out.

"Bye, Raymond," Lexi said.

Before Raymond could answer, Joseph shoved into him, knocking him into a chair.

"Watch it," Joseph growled, and stormed past him. "Hey, Lexi, wait up!" he called in an entirely different tone. Raymond was pleased to see Lexi roll her eyes and march out of the classroom without answering.

The next morning, Raymond woke up feeling nervous. He had worked with Lexi before in class, but there was something entirely different about the prospect of being alone with her.

When Lexi asked him if they were still on for the afternoon, he nodded and smiled but didn't say anything. He tried to appear as if he were focusing and taking notes during Mr. Rosen's lesson on symbiotic relationships, but he barely heard a word of what Mr. Rosen was saying. He forgot to answer the question of the day in English and kept tripping over his feet in gym.

When the final bell rang in art, Raymond said goodbye to Harlin and made his way back through the school. Most of the students were filing out and into the courtyard either to wait for their parents or to catch their bus. Raymond pushed past them and into the boys' bathroom. Thankfully, it was empty. He looked in the mirror and ran his fingers through his hair. The sun had lightened his sandy-blond waves, which had now grown past his ears. He brushed his hair back, trying to undo the knots with his fingers. He sniffed himself.

"Get it together," he told his reflection. He splashed some water on his face and pulled the brown paper towels from the holder and dried off. "She's just a friend." He walked out the door and made his way to the library.

He looked around but didn't see Lexi right away. He thought that maybe she'd stood him up. Then he spotted her red hair. She was sitting at a table over in the corner of the library.

Raymond walked over to the table and took the seat opposite her.

"Hey, Raymond," she said cheerfully. "I almost thought you weren't going to make it."

Raymond smiled. He felt more relaxed now that he was actually there.

"I checked out all the books on teeth that I could find but there aren't that many. I asked my dad if we could use some of the teeth he pulls and he said we could. I think we should use the clean ones, though, to keep it controlled." They had decided to do an experiment on decay. They were planning to use drinks with different sugar contents to see which teeth became more stained over time.

"That's great!" Raymond said.

"Yes, but we might have to wait until next week. My dad said he doesn't have that many extractions scheduled so it might take a few days to collect them."

"That's fine," Raymond said, and shrugged. "We have a few weeks, right? I figure we just need long enough to actually see the stains. What do you think, about a week?" They were going to drop the teeth into containers with the drinks and monitor them each day.

"Seven days would probably be enough," Lexi agreed. They spent the rest of the afternoon deciding on what drinks to use and looking up their sugar contents on the computer. Raymond took diligent notes in his notebook, keeping track of all their research and plans.

It was four thirty when Ms. Amber, the school librarian, came over to tell them she was going home. They packed up their bags and Lexi waited with Raymond while he renewed the *Boy Scouts Handbook*. Ms. Amber tsked at the book's frayed edges. Throwing it into the snow hadn't helped its condition. Raymond promised to be more careful.

On the way out, Raymond stopped at the door.

"I'll see you tomorrow, then," he said, trying to sound casual.

"You aren't coming outside?" she asked.

"I need to grab my math book from my cubby."

Lexi accepted the excuse without question. "Want to meet again at the same time next week? I should have the teeth by then."

Raymond felt his whole body grow warm. "Sounds good," he agreed. Lexi pushed through the front door and was gone.

On Friday, Ms. Marcus passed out a story by Edgar Allan Poe. It was the second one they'd read by Poe that week. Raymond was doodling sketches in his notebook of animal traps to try building after school. Although it was months away, he worried about the summer months and what his food supplies might look like when the school was closed. He couldn't rely on Hank or Rosie for steady food and while the river usually provided, it wasn't consistent. He would start with traps and, if they didn't work, then he'd figure something else out.

"Ugh, another one of these weird stories," a boy behind Raymond complained. The comment was loud enough for Ms. Marcus to hear but she ignored it.

There was a little biography at the top of the page and Ms. Marcus asked a girl in the back of the room to read it aloud. Raymond tucked away his notebook and tried to pay attention. He was surprised to hear that Edgar Allan Poe had experienced so much tragedy in his life. He had lost everyone he ever loved.

"No wonder he wrote things that were so dark," a girl in the front row said. "His life was basically nothing but death and abandonment."

"Yeah, I mean he was alone," another girl said. "It's so depressing." Raymond couldn't help but take their comments personally. After reading the biography, he felt a certain kinship with the author. It wasn't his fault everyone had died or left him.

Ms. Marcus listened quietly and then said, "Sometimes there are worse things than being alone." Raymond looked at his teacher. Stigs had said the exact same thing to him. There was a sadness on Ms. Marcus's face as she began reading aloud but soon all thoughts of Stigs and Ms. Marcus and animal traps melted away as Raymond became totally absorbed by the words in front of him.

At the end of class, Ms. Marcus passed out copies of the poem "Annabel Lee" (also written by Poe) and told them to annotate it for homework. Raymond groaned with the rest of the class. More homework. His homework load had reached an all-time high and he stayed huddled up by the fire each night, working until nightfall. It had been a sunny but cold week back to school and Raymond hadn't been able to go fishing. He had gone to sleep hungry and even with his coat, fur hat, and sleeping bag, he struggled to keep from shivering. Homework would just have to wait today.

"Let's set a trap!" Raymond announced to Hank and Rosie when he got back to the hollow that afternoon.

Raymond walked along the creek in search of large rocks. On the survival show he'd watched with his father, a lot of the contestants set their own traps. But it was so long ago that he'd seen the show, and he'd never actually done it on his own, so he really couldn't remember all the instructions. But he remembered the overall gist, so he figured it couldn't hurt to try.

His plan was to prop up a heavy rock using sticks, place bait beneath it, and hope an animal would knock the rock over when they went for the bait. It wasn't the most sophisticated idea but it was the only thing he could think of. The *Boy Scouts Handbook* offered lots of information on identifying animals and their tracks but not a lot in the way of advice on trapping them.

He bent to pry a large rock from the freezing creek bed.

The rock was way too light and came up easily. Raymond dropped it back in the water. He needed a rock heavy enough to kill a small animal. Finally, he found a large, flat rock that he thought must weigh around twenty-five pounds. He pried it from the water and slung it up on dry land. He dragged the rock to a fairly flat area in the woods where he had once seen a field mouse. Rosie jogged along behind him, doing her best to keep up. She had downright refused to stay in the camp alone. Hank had come along at first but quickly lost interest and started chasing squirrels.

"Hey, we'll take one of those, Hank!" Raymond yelled after him. He pulled his prepared sticks from his back pocket. He had three main sticks and one small toggle, all lightweight but sturdy enough to hold up a rock. He set the Y-shaped stick in the ground. He situated the next stick in between the Y. It would act as a lever. He had tied a length of fishing line to the lever and on the other end of the line he attached the toggle. He propped the rock on its side and positioned it over the lever, looping the toggle around the post. Finally, he laid the third stick beneath the rock, wedged between its base and holding the toggle in place at the other end.

He let go. The top rock smashed down, pinning his pinkie finger to the ground. "Arghhhh!" he screamed, and Rosie darted back. He pulled his finger from the wreckage and kicked the wrecked trap. He held his hand gingerly. The nail on his pinkie finger was already filling with blood. It was cracked down the middle.

Raymond walked to the creek and through gritted teeth

put his hand into the cold water. Even in the cold water, his finger pulsed with heat. He looked back at the fallen trap with a new determination.

"I will set that trap today, Rosie." Rosie lay down to watch.

After several attempts, two more smashed fingers, and some very colorful language, he got the rock to stay up on its own. Raymond tossed a few crackers under the trap and stepped back to admire his work. It felt highly unlikely that this trap would ever yield anything. Still, there was a certain sense of accomplishment in having completed it, and he suddenly wished someone was around to acknowledge it.

Chapter Sixteen

Raymond woke up early the next morning. In the smoky light of the day, he checked his trap. The crackers were gone and the trap was still standing. He couldn't help but feel a little disappointed. He reset it and added another cracker. Then he headed to the school to scavenge the dumpsters before going to meet Stigs at the river. The snow had melted away but the ground was hard as ice. He managed to save an unopened box of expired breakfast bars, about a dozen oranges, and his best find yet: a huge unopened bag of Quaker Instant Grits. He stowed them away in the hollow, eating a breakfast bar and tossing one to Rosie. He pocketed an orange to eat on the way. He grabbed his fishing gear and headed to the river.

Hank had left camp the night before and was still missing this morning, but Raymond had learned that week that coyotes often walked miles away from their homes, hunting. He hoped Hank would be back soon. He liked having the coyote around. The noises of the woods at night were a little less intimidating with a coyote sleeping outside the hollow. Rosie was in good spirits, obviously pleased with Hank's absence. They stopped by the river to collect the contents of Raymond's minnow traps. Then they walked back through the woods and up to the road. They crossed over the bridge and entered the woods on the other side.

Stigs was already waiting at the water in his usual spot and Rosie jogged ahead to greet him.

"I see that leg is doing all right," Stigs said, rubbing the dog's head. He pulled some jerky from his pocket and Rosie accepted, licking his hands. "What took you so long?" he asked Raymond. "I've already caught three fish."

"Three?" Raymond said happily, opening his tackle box to bait his hook. He cast his line and went to stand by the old man, who was seated on a log, re-baiting a hook.

"How's school?" Stigs asked, handing Raymond a thermos of hot chocolate.

"School is school." Raymond shrugged. He took a long swig, relishing the warmth.

"That old hat looks good."

"Yeah," said Raymond, adjusting the earflaps. "Thanks."

Stigs grunted and cast his line in the river. The pair fished for a few hours. They didn't talk much and Raymond was just fine with that. He caught a good-size catfish, and Stigs helped him clean it, showing Raymond how to correctly fillet the fish to get rid of all the bones. He carefully cut the fish around the dorsal fins and then down its back, using the spine as a guide. Stigs was a patient teacher, and Raymond was happy for the pointers.

When the sun was high, Stigs unwrapped two sandwiches, offering one to Raymond. "You keeping fed?" he asked.

"I am," said Raymond without looking at the old man. He took the sandwich and ate it slowly, feeling Stigs's eyes on him.

"Your folks make it back?"

Raymond nodded. Stigs wasn't exactly prying but Raymond knew that he wasn't convinced by his assurances that everything was fine at home.

"Thanks for the knife," he said, changing the subject.

"Glad you can use it," said Stigs. "It needed a good home. How's that friend of yours that you told me about?"

"Harlin? He's good. He's Harlin." Raymond smiled. "Why?"

"I know his father if I'm thinking about the same kid. He played ball with my son growing up. Had a hard time, that one."

"Harlin? Or his father?" Raymond asked.

"His father," Stigs said. Raymond knew that Harlin lived with his grandmother, his father's mother. Harlin had mentioned his father a few times but nothing major. He'd never really asked Harlin much about his family, mostly because he didn't want Harlin asking him about his. They seemed to have a mutual understanding that way.

After lunch, Stigs stood. "I better be getting back. You staying?"

"Yeah, for a while," said Raymond. He was hoping to get enough fish to try out a new technique to preserve the ones he caught.

"Suit yourself," said Stigs, packing up his gear.

"See you next weekend?" asked Raymond. Stigs grunted and patted Rosie's head. Then he turned and walked through the woods without another word. Raymond stayed at the river until close to dark, only catching one more small catfish. Then he packed up his gear and went back to camp.

Ignoring his book bag full of homework, Raymond made a fire and prepared his fish, setting them on the A-frame to roast. Then he walked to the creek to fill his can with water. He carried the can of water back to camp and set it on the coals.

He waited as the fish roasted, turning them patiently, warming his stiff fingers by the flames. When the water in the can was hot, he poured in grits, holding the bag carefully. That week, Raymond had whittled a spoon, and he stirred the grits with it, pulling the can from the fire to cool. He would work on a fork next and he thought maybe even a set of tongs might be nice.

He sat with Rosie, eating roasted fish and grits as the sun set. He cleaned up at the creek just as a light snow started to fall. He heated river stones in the fire and tucked them into the sleeping bag for extra warmth, a tip he thanked the Boy Scouts for. He adjusted the fur hat, tying it firmly under his chin, and crawled into the hollow. He hung the curtain of ferns in the opening and pulled Rosie close, trying to burrow into the sleeping bag. Rosie licked his cheek and he closed his eyes and said a silent prayer that the snow would be a light one.

On Sunday, Raymond washed his clothes in the creek, using the last of his soap, and laid them by the fire to dry. He would have to get another bar soon. The snowfall the night before had been just a dusting but he was careful not to slip on the frosted river stones as he worked. He cleaned himself as well, pulling his clothing off piece by piece, nearly freezing to death in the process.

There was still no sign of Hank as Raymond tried to finish his English homework that evening. The temperature had dropped again, and the light snow was now crunchy under his feet. Raymond was having trouble getting warm again after his creek bath so he pulled his river stones from the fire and tucked them in his sleeping bag again. He crawled in and tried to read from the Boy Scouts manual before bed, hoping the sleeping bag would warm his bones. Rosie was curled against Raymond, sleeping soundly. He tucked the book away and tried to join her. His body begged for sleep but he just couldn't relax. He tried to wiggle his toes but couldn't tell if they were actually moving. He began to shiver again. The shiver quickly turned to shaking and it became so uncontrollable that Rosie woke up and began licking his face. When he could no longer stand it, he pulled himself from the hollow and tried to steady his arms enough to build a fire back up in the darkness.

It was difficult to carry the kindling. He had trouble gripping the branches without shaking and kept dropping the matches in his loose grip, so he abandoned the matches and used the birch tree bark. The fire relit easily from the already hot coals. Raymond added stick after stick, limb after limb to the flames, using his entire firewood supply. He pulled the sleeping bag from the hollow and laid it on the ground so close to the fire that he worried it might burn. Then he crawled in and tried to relax his body. He took deep breaths, his teeth chattering as he did. He felt the heat from the fire on his cheeks and nose, almost cutting him against the cold. Rosie whined and Raymond opened the sleeping bag, letting her crawl in. He closed his eyes and with the warmth came sleep.

Ms. Marcus passed back *The Outsiders* theme essays in English the next day. Raymond looked at the large C- at the top of the paper. He had never received anything lower than a B in school. There was a note at the bottom of the page.

See me after class.—Ms. M

He looked up at his teacher. She was staring right at him and he looked away quickly and tucked the essay into his bag.

Raymond turned in his half-completed "Annabel Lee" annotations from the weekend. When class was over, Raymond stayed seated in his chair while the other kids filed out for their next class. Ms. Marcus came and sat down at the desk in front of him. She turned to face him. He looked at his desk.

"Raymond?" she said quietly. "I thought we talked about your grades slipping before the break ended. I really expected you to turn in your best work on this essay."

"That was my best work," Raymond said, but even he knew he was lying. He'd written it the night before break ended and it was sloppy and scattered. He shook his head a little and sighed. "Break just got really . . . well, busy. I thought I did okay." He continued to look at his desk. He could feel Ms. Marcus's eyes on him.

"Is that what you're going for now, Raymond? Just okay? When I'm confident that you could do so much better?"

Ms. Marcus was right, but that essay was the best he could manage right now and that would just have to be good enough. There were more important things for Raymond to be worrying about. He rubbed his knuckles and tried to focus on the little specks of brown on his desk.

Ms. Marcus sighed. "What's going on, Raymond? Middle school can be pretty tough years. You seem so much older than most of the kids your age. Smarter, even." She laughed, and Raymond felt himself relax a little. "That's why it seems so odd that you would turn something in so mediocre." And then she asked the question that teachers always ask: "Is there anything I can do to help?"

Raymond looked at Ms. Marcus. He shook his head, wishing that there *was* something she could do to help. "No ma'am. I'm fine," he said. "I'll try to do better from now on."

A crease formed between Ms. Marcus's eyebrows. The way she was looking at him reminded Raymond of how Stigs looked at him sometimes. He thought she was going to start asking him more questions but instead she said, "Okay, Raymond. I'm going to write you a pass for gym." And just like that, Raymond was dismissed.

When Raymond got back to his camp that afternoon, a haggard-looking Hank was lying in the leaves, sunbathing.

Rosie was standing over him, and Raymond thought that if Rosie could talk, she would be giving him a lecture on cleanliness.

"Hank!" Raymond called happily, and the coyote stretched and arched his back, rolled in the leaves, and wagged his tail playfully. "Where've you been?" Raymond had missed the coyote. Hank jumped up and did a few small leaps. Raymond laughed. "I see not much has changed, then." Rosie made a groaning noise against Raymond. "I see you, Rosie," Raymond told her, scratching her ears.

Raymond walked to check his trap. After several days with no success, he had moved the trap to a location closer to camp and upgraded his bait to some leftover slices of orange. The trap was still standing and the orange slices were gone. "Sneaky," Raymond said, wondering what type of animal had removed whole orange slices without setting off the trap. He grabbed another orange from the hollow. He squeezed some of the juice around the trap and then carefully laid a piece of the orange back under the rock and ate the rest.

Raymond spent the afternoon doubling the insulation in the hollow. He hung another curtain of ferns in the mouth of the hollow and padded the floor with soft moss pulled off rocks, more ferns, and pine straw. He was already wearing all his clothing to bed. He convinced himself that the shivering was due to hunger. That it wasn't too cold outside, he just wasn't getting enough food. He needed calories. He needed *meat*. He checked his trap again. Still nothing.

Raymond looked at his fishing pole. He sighed. Mr. Brewer had assigned thirty math problems for tonight. He cooked grits and peeled oranges for dinner and worked on his math homework. "How about a rabbit, Hank?" he asked, but Hank was already asleep.

Chapter Seventeen

Raymond sat in the cafeteria eating his breakfast of French toast sticks. He looked around for Harlin, who was usually there by now. He was almost finished with his milk when a few kids came running in. The kids went straight to Ms. Marcus, and she hurried out of the cafeteria into the courtyard. Raymond wondered what was going on. He stood to throw his trash away and was almost to the trash can when Lexi came through the cafeteria doors. She looked around and then her eyes found Raymond.

Raymond knew immediately that something was wrong. Lexi made a beeline across the cafeteria to him. He tried not to panic. *This is not about me,* he thought. *Nobody knows. Nobody knows.* He racked his brain. Did he forget to stomp out the fire this morning? Did Hank follow him to school? He could feel his heart racing and then Lexi was right in front of him.

"It's Harlin," she said. "He's . . ." She shook her head. "Just come, okay?" She grabbed Raymond by the arm and he allowed himself to be dragged from the cafeteria.

Outside, there were students everywhere. Harlin was standing in the middle of the courtyard, somehow alone in a sea of students, staring at a man who Ms. Marcus was now desperately trying to calm down.

"It's his dad," Lexi whispered to Raymond, her voice full of angst. But even if she hadn't said anything, Raymond would've known by the look on Harlin's face. Raymond wasn't sure what he should do but he knew he couldn't just stand there with Lexi, watching it happen. He pushed past the crowd of students and went to stand with Harlin. Harlin made eye contact with Raymond.

Harlin's father was pacing the breezeway in front of the school. He was shouting for Harlin to come over but Ms. Marcus was standing in front of him, asking him to lower his voice, trying to get him to sit down. This seemed to make Harlin's father more agitated. He ran his fingers through his hair and gripped at his shirt.

Raymond couldn't do anything but stand there. He could hear a voice, Lexi's maybe, behind him, yelling at the other students to go away, to stop staring. He thought maybe he should yell too but he felt speechless and he knew that no matter what, he wouldn't leave Harlin.

Then Mrs. Harding came running out of the office with Mr. Brewer. Within minutes, Raymond heard sirens and then two police cars were pulling into the school parking lot.

"Harlin!" his father was screaming. "He's right there!" he yelled at the cops and Raymond could see spit hanging from his mouth. The cops handcuffed Harlin's father and put him in the back seat, and Raymond could only see the outline of his head as the police car with him in it pulled out of the parking lot.

Mrs. Harding marched over to clear the rest of the courtyard of students, and then Ms. Marcus was standing in front of them. "Come on, you two," she said quietly. She put her arm around

Harlin, who let go of Raymond's hand. Raymond looked down. He hadn't even realized that he'd been holding it.

Raymond and Harlin were seated for the second time that year in Mrs. Harding's office. Only this time, they were offered water and peppermints. "I'm so sorry, Harlin," Ms. Marcus said.

Harlin nodded and shrugged. He took a sip of his water.

Mrs. Harding walked by. "Ms. Marcus, the police officers would like a statement from you," she said.

"All right," Ms. Marcus replied, looking back at Raymond and Harlin like she wanted to say something but didn't know what. Then she shook her head and walked out.

Mrs. Harding stepped into the room. "Harlin, I'm going to call your grandmother to come and pick you up," she said. "I think it might be best if you don't go to classes today. Raymond, why don't you wait with him? I'll give you a pass back to class later."

"Yes ma'am," Raymond responded. Mrs. Harding left, pulling the door of her office closed behind her.

"It's my birthday today," Harlin told Raymond. Raymond looked at his friend. "That's why he came. 'Cause today's my birthday. He does this on holidays."

Raymond wasn't sure what to say so he didn't say anything.

"He gets sick," Harlin said. He was concentrating on his cup of water. Raymond could feel the familiar lump in his throat. He swallowed. *There are worse things than being alone*, Raymond thought. And then he did something he had never done before.

"My parents leave me all the time," he said. His voice was surprisingly steady. "I haven't seen them in over a month."

Just then, the door opened and Mrs. Harding stuck her head in. "Your grandmother is on the way, Harlin. She'll be here any minute." She left the door open when she left. Apart from the office noises and Mrs. Bradsher answering the phone, the room was completely silent.

After what seemed like a very long time, Mrs. Harding stuck her head in again. "She's here."

Harlin set his cup down and stood up. "Bye, Raymond."

Raymond smiled at his friend. "See ya, Harlin."

Mrs. Harding returned with Raymond's pass. "Mr. Brewer knows you'll be late today." Raymond thanked her and headed to his class. As he walked by the school's front doors, he saw Harlin's grandmother hugging Harlin. Raymond smiled, glad that Harlin had someone to hug. He knew he should be worried that Harlin would tell someone about his parents, but somehow Raymond knew he wouldn't.

The rest of the school day was torture for Raymond. Harlin's father was the only thing anybody seemed to be talking about. In the hall, Jeremy Wallace was loud enough for everyone to hear. "If I had a dad like that, I'd never show my face again."

Raymond felt anger surge through him but before he could do anything, Lexi was there.

"Why don't you shut your tiny mouth, Jeremy," she said.

"Aw, Lexi," he said. "I was only kidding."

"Well, take your jokes somewhere else," she said. Jeremy smiled but Lexi shook her head.

Then Joseph Banker knocked Jeremy's shoulder. "Yeah, Jeremy. Go somewhere else." Jeremy looked at his friend, confused. Jeremy walked off, pushing past Raymond and shooting him a look that could cut through ice. Raymond rolled his eyes and followed the rest of the class into science and sat down.

"Hey," Lexi said to Raymond. "Is Harlin okay?"

"I don't think so," Raymond said. "But he will be. Harlin's pretty tough."

"Yes," said Lexi. Her voice was sad and she lowered it even more, careful of who was listening. "This isn't the first time this has happened."

Raymond wondered how many times Harlin's father had shown up before now.

Lexi sighed and then perked up like she had just remembered something. "Hey, I got the teeth. Want to meet tomorrow after school?"

"That sounds good," Raymond said, but he felt distracted. Mr. Rosen told the class to quiet down then, as he turned on a movie about conducting experiments. The class took notes for the rest of the period, but Raymond stared out the window, worrying about his friend.

After school, Raymond collapsed into a pile of leaves outside of the hollow. He felt like he'd been holding his breath all day and could finally let it go. Tears poured from his eyes, and he pulled his knees to his forehead and buried his face in his arms. It wasn't fair. Harlin didn't deserve parents like he had. Raymond took a deep shaking breath and thought of his own parents. He squeezed his eyes shut.

Within minutes, Rosie found him. She dug her nose under his elbow and tried to wedge herself between his knees. Raymond let out a strangled laugh and allowed her to wriggle in. He hugged Rosie and took a deep breath. *I can do this,* he thought. He exhaled. He leaned against the hollow and looked around. No Hank today.

"Come on, Rosie," he said. He stood up and they checked his trap. The rock lay flat on the ground and the sticks were scattered. Raymond held his breath and lifted the rock. Underneath lay a squirrel. There was no doubt that he had had a quick death and Raymond quietly thanked the animal. He turned to his dog. "This one is all yours, girl," he said.

The next day at breakfast, Raymond sat eating his ham biscuit, checking the door every few seconds for Harlin. Finally, he saw him. Harlin was wearing his usual oversize racing shirt. After a few minutes, Harlin appeared standing by the table with his breakfast tray, looking awkwardly at Raymond.

"What are you doing? Aren't you going to sit down?" Raymond asked.

Harlin let out an exaggerated breath and sat down across from Raymond. "I wasn't sure you'd still want to sit with me after yesterday. Usually scares folks off a bit." He took a bite of biscuit.

"I don't scare easily," Raymond said.

"Me either." Harlin grinned and sipped his milk. "Sorry about your parents. They been gone for a while, huh?"

Raymond shifted uncomfortably in his seat. He glanced behind his shoulder to make sure nobody was around.

"Not so loud, Harlin. Please," Raymond said.

"Sorry," he said, and then in a very serious tone asked, "But Ray, what have you been eating?"

"Fish mostly," Raymond answered honestly.

Harlin nodded. "Maybe I can bring you some supplies? Just tell me what you need."

"Thank you, Harlin. I'll let you know." Raymond knew he probably wouldn't ask Harlin for anything, but there was a sense of relief knowing he could if he needed to.

"I don't know what I'd do if I was alone for that long. Probably eat cake for breakfast every morning—"

"Harlin?" Raymond cut in.

"Yeah?"

"Can we talk about something else?"

Harlin leaned back and took another bite of his biscuit without missing a beat. "You see the race last night?" he asked, talking with his mouth full. Raymond shook his head. He was happy to have his friend back.

Chapter Eighteen

In the library that afternoon, Lexi arrived carrying containers that she set down on the table. "Mr. Rosen just said to clean them out before we give them back. I got the drinks too," she said, pulling the bottles from her bag. They filled each container, measuring the contents. Lexi took a picture as they dropped a tooth in each one. "I asked Ms. Amber if we could leave them here in the library. Ya know, so we can monitor them each day? I'll take them home over the weekend unless you want to?" She looked at Raymond.

"I can take them," he said. He wanted to pull his weight. Lexi had done most of the work so far.

When they were finished, Lexi made a spreadsheet to record their data, and Raymond wrote out their hypothesis on notebook paper. He wasn't so good with computers, having never actually owned one. His parents had a tablet once but that had only been good for playing games. His dad had stepped on it one night when he came in late. He promised to get it fixed for Raymond but he never did.

"How long have you known Joseph?" Raymond asked.

"For forever," Lexi said, clicking away at the computer keys. "How about this?" His eyes breezed over the screen.

"Looks great to me," he said. Raymond didn't want to push the Joseph topic but he was curious. Sometimes it seemed like Lexi and Joseph were friends. They had worked together in class before. But other times, Lexi seemed just as annoyed with Joseph as Raymond was. Raymond didn't have much experience with friends, so he couldn't tell if Lexi was friends with Joseph or not. Raymond certainly was not.

Lexi looked at Raymond. "Our moms are best friends so I've known him my whole life. Mostly I can't stand him. He used to call me Freckleface and dunk my pigtails in glue when we were in elementary school." She rolled her eyes. "Anyway, I know he bugs you. Just ignore him. That's what I try to do."

Raymond tried to smile.

When it was almost four thirty, Lexi packed up her stuff. "Well, I'd better go," she said. "My little sister has dance practice tonight and my mom gets upset if we're late."

"I'll just finish this up and then head home," Raymond told her, pretending to write something in his notebook.

"See you tomorrow, Raymond."

"Bye," he said, waving awkwardly.

On Friday, Raymond packed the containers in his book bag carefully, promising to take notes over the weekend. They were finished with the science project for the day so Raymond and Lexi helped Ms. Amber shelf the returned books until Mrs. Bradsher walked into the library.

"Lexi," she said, "your mom's here. She's waiting in the office for you."

Lexi thanked Mrs. Bradsher, who walked to the checkout counter to talk to Ms. Amber. Lexi grabbed her things. "Bye, Raymond. See you Monday."

On Saturday, Raymond woke up to a cacophony of birdsong. His legs and back were stiff, and he groaned inside the sleeping bag. He crawled from the hollow and stretched. Rosie jumped down behind him. Hank was leaping around the camp with his eyes toward the treetops. Raymond wasn't used to hearing so many birds in the middle of January and he couldn't help but take it as a good omen. Sun crept through the trees and Raymond soaked in the warmth of it. The days were manageable but the nights were still bitter cold, even with Raymond's adjustments to the hollow. He wouldn't miss these winter months one bit. For now, though, the snow had at least melted and the sun was out.

He brushed his teeth and lifted the nape of his hoodie to smell himself. It had been a week since he'd bathed in the cold water and he wasn't prepared to spend another night shivering uncontrollably. No, he would have to figure something else out.

He pulled the containers from his book bag and took careful notes on each tooth. Then he tucked them back in his bag.

Raymond stopped to collect his minnows and was the first to arrive at his and Stigs's usual fishing spot. He sat on the log and began baiting his hook, waiting for Stigs to arrive. Rosie heard him coming first and jogged to meet him. Stigs trudged through the brush and lightly kicked the side of Raymond's shoe in a greeting before sitting down on the log himself.

"Brought you some eggs," he said, and he handed over a milk jug full of eggs. Stigs had cut the top off the jug but the handle was still on the plastic container. Raymond inspected the jug and Stigs smiled. "Makes for an easy basket. Waste not and all that . . ." He shrugged. Raymond smiled.

"This is a ton of eggs." There had to be at least twenty eggs inside the jug.

"Well, the girls have been busy and there's always more than I can eat. I usually take some over to the Veterans Affairs in Commerce but I thought I'd bring them to you this week instead. You'll have to come up for a visit soon and see the chickens," Stigs said. "They're starting to miss you."

Raymond nodded. "I will. Thank you."

"You're welcome. So, how's school?"

"It's okay," Raymond said. He set the eggs down and instantly felt his mood change with the question. "It's just so much work all the time. And now there's a science fair project on top of everything else."

"Science fairs still look the same as they always did? Exploding volcanoes and all?" Stigs asked.

"You can come see for yourself," Raymond answered, and laughed.

"At the school?" Stigs asked.

"Yes. You remember how to get there, don't you?" Raymond smiled.

Stigs grinned. "Haven't been there in a while," he said quietly, his voice trailing off like he was remembering. "I never much cared for school. Just went for the food."

Raymond shook his head. "It's not that I don't want to learn because I do. I actually like school. There are just more important things than doing homework all the time."

"Like what?" Stigs asked.

Raymond sat there with his mouth shut. He had a list a mile long of things that were more important to him than homework but he couldn't say any of them out loud. So instead, he grinned and said, "Like fishing."

Stigs chuckled, and then something tugged on Raymond's line that almost ripped the entire pole from his grip. Raymond leapt up, leaning into the rod.

"Easy," Stigs coached, jumping to his feet. "She's a big one, all right. Careful now, don't jerk her around. Take your time."

Raymond dug his feet into the sandy bank. He reeled the line and took a few steps, reeled and stepped. Finally, he pulled in the biggest bass that he had ever seen. It was nearly sixteen inches and had to weigh at least eight pounds, maybe more.

"She's a beaut!" Stigs cheered.

Raymond hadn't noticed that Rosie was barking, but now that he had the fish it was all he could hear.

"She's excited. She's probably never seen a fish this big. I don't think I've ever seen a fish this big. You ought to mount her," Stigs suggested.

"Mount her?" Raymond said, shocked. "What would I do

with a mounted fish? I'm gonna eat her!" Rosie barked again and Stigs laughed so hard, Raymond couldn't help but join in.

That afternoon, Raymond cooked a feast. He filleted the fish and roasted it one half at a time. Just one half was a huge amount of meat and it was too much to roast on his A-frame at once. He set half aside while he roasted. Hank showed up just in time for dinner and Raymond had to keep shooing him away from the uncooked fish. It had been a clear day and Raymond shed his hat and coat while he cooked, enjoying the ease of fifty-degree weather.

He cooked egg after egg in a cleaned-out tuna fish can masquerading as a tiny frying pan, one by one, offering them to Rosie and Hank with chunks of roasted fish. He boiled water in his ravioli can and poured in grits. The trio ate happily until all the food was gone. He tucked the remaining ten eggs in the back of the hollow with his cache of oranges from earlier in the week. He walked to the creek and cleaned his wooden spoon and fork in the water. Maybe tomorrow he would make a pair of tongs. He washed out his cooking cans and stored them all under the lean-to with the kindling. Then, even though the sun hadn't set, Raymond tucked his warmed river stones into his sleeping bag, crawled into the hollow with a full belly, and fell asleep smiling.

Chapter Nineteen

On Monday morning, Raymond checked his cubby. He pulled out a pink flyer advertising that on the first Friday in February, the school would be hosting the semi-formal dance. He tucked his books in his bag and threw the flyer in the trash.

It seemed the whole school was completely absorbed with talk of the semi-formal. Even the teachers seemed excited. Raymond couldn't understand for the life of him why anyone would want to go to a dance.

"You going to the dance?" Harlin asked him that afternoon.

"I doubt it," said Raymond. Going to a dance was about the last thing he wanted to do. Besides, he didn't have anything to wear even if he did want to go.

"Might be fun," Harlin said, and his ears reddened.

Raymond couldn't help himself. "Maybe you could ask that girl from the Jamboree to go with you? Lexi's friend? What was her name?"

Harlin's complexion turned from pink to bright red at the suggestion and he shook his head.

"Come on," said Raymond, grinning. "Couldn't hurt to ask."

"Naw. A girl like that would never go to a dance with the likes of me," said Harlin. "Maybe you could ask Lexi?" Now it was Raymond's turn to blush.

Harlin thumbed the colored pencils on the table. After

a minute, he sighed and picked up a red pencil. "I probably won't go either. Was a dumb idea." Harlin didn't mention the dance again but Raymond knew he was still thinking about it as he sketched the flower vase in the middle of the table.

The science project was almost finished. That afternoon in the library, Lexi used fancy lettering to sketch out their project title and Ms. Amber let them print their work to paste to the display board. All that was left was to record the final results.

"Oh, and I can't meet tomorrow or Wednesday," Lexi said as she packed up her things for the day. "I'm trying out for the cross-country team."

"I didn't know you were a runner," said Raymond.

"I'm not." She laughed. "My parents think it will look good on my college applications if I play a sport. I figure, how hard can it be to run?"

"I guess you'll find out." He liked how easy it was to talk to Lexi. "I can take notes and type up the results while you're at tryouts," he said. "And that will leave us Thursday to finalize it all." Friday was a teacher workday and the school would be closed Monday for the Martin Luther King Jr. holiday. Most students were happy about the long weekend. Except for Raymond. That was one more day he would have to feed himself.

The temperature that week was almost bearable. Raymond slept through the night without shivering, and he was more than happy about it. His body didn't ache like it usually did and his whole attitude improved. He knew it would inevitably get cold again, but he was enjoying the not-quite-freezing temperatures while they lasted.

The creek water was still ice cold, but he found a way to clean himself efficiently without freezing to death. He had managed to pocket a half-used bar of soap from the boys' locker room and used Stigs's milk jug basket to collect water from the creek. Then he warmed the water in the jug the same way that he warmed his sleeping bag at night, pulling heated river stones from the fire with his newly whittled tongs and dropping them in the water.

Raymond checked the teeth and took notes while Lexi tried out for cross-country. And on Thursday, Lexi told Raymond that she had made the team.

"That's great!" Raymond said, trying to keep his voice down in the library.

"Not really," she said. "We have to practice practically every day. So I won't be able to meet you after school for a while." Raymond felt his chest swell. He had assumed that once the project was over, they wouldn't be meeting after school anymore anyway. He was very pleased to hear that Lexi still wanted to.

Just before four thirty, Mrs. Bradsher showed up to let Lexi know her mom was ready. She and Raymond said their goodbyes and he stowed the display board and the containers in the closet. Raymond had never participated in a science fair before so he wasn't totally sure, but their project was a winner in his eyes.

"How are you doing, Raymond?" Ms. Amber asked when he got to the checkout counter. "Are you liking it at River Mill?" Mrs. Bradsher adjusted her hair and leaned on the counter, waiting for Ms. Amber to finish and ignoring Raymond completely.

"Yes ma'am," he said. "I like it a lot."

"How are your classes? Are you keeping up with the work? You are in Ms. Marcus's advanced English class, aren't you?"

"They're good," he said. "And yes ma'am. She's a good teacher."

"I'm so glad to hear that," said Ms. Amber. "Are you checking something out today?"

"I think so. Do you have any books about hunting and trapping?" Raymond asked, trying to sound casual.

Ms. Amber walked Raymond to a shelf on the other side of the library. "That's a pretty popular topic, actually. You should find some good options over here in the nonfiction section. But look quickly, the library is closing soon."

"Yes ma'am. Thank you," he said. Raymond began thumbing through the books on the shelf. Then he decided that he might like to read something a bit more upbeat. He headed over to a section marked "Survival Stories."

He selected a book and went to check it out.

"Did you find something, dear?" Ms. Amber asked.

Raymond nodded and set the copy of *Hatchet* on the desk.

Ms. Amber checked it out and handed the book to Raymond. "Enjoy the long weekend," she said.

He tucked the book into his bag and left the library. When he made it to the side door, he glanced down the hall.

Ms. Marcus's light was still on in her classroom. Raymond considered stopping in to say hello but thought better of it. He pushed the door open and quietly slipped around the back of the school and into the woods.

Back at the hollow, an eager Rosie sniffed at Raymond's pockets. He had forgotten to save some of his breakfast and lunch. He checked the back of the hollow. It was nearly empty except for a brown banana and a half-eaten Pop-Tart, which he offered to Rosie and she grudgingly ate. He had been so preoccupied this week with Lexi and the science project that he had let his food stores totally deplete. He checked his trap and found it set off but empty. It was too late in the day to go fishing and that wasn't a guarantee anyway.

Once it got dark he headed back in the direction of the school to check the dumpsters. It was Thursday and he knew by now that the trash trucks came on Tuesday and Thursday mornings, so anything he found would still be fresh from the day. From the edge of the baseball field, he could see Ms. Marcus's classroom still lit up. Her car was parked in the side lot, so Raymond thought he would be in the clear at the dumpsters on the other side of the school.

He continued around the back of the school and waited just inside the tree line for a few minutes to be sure nobody else had stayed late. All was quiet and dark, aside from the overhead light in the front parking lot. Raymond could hear it buzzing as it blinked on and off. He darted for the dumpster, and heaved the top open and pulled himself in.

They had served macaroni that day, and Raymond gagged

as he flung leftover noodles from his hands. He found an unopened bag of potato chips and half a loaf of white bread. The outside was coated with pasta but the inside appeared unscathed. He wiped the bread bag off as best he could and closed the trash bag. He lifted himself out of the dumpster and tried to land softly on the gravel below. He shut the lid. He peered around the corner of the school before darting back into the woods.

When he made it to the baseball field under the cover of trees, he checked the school again. Ms. Marcus's light was off and her car was no longer in the side lot. Feeling nervous, he ran back to the hollow as fast as he could.

It rained all of Thursday night and into Friday. Raymond stayed in the hollow with Rosie, eating potato chips and reading. He had widened the lean-to recently to include a sheltered spot for Hank. But by Friday night, even Hank was restless, and he trotted out of the camp in the pouring rain.

Raymond was starving by Saturday morning after only eating potato chip sandwiches the day before. Thankful for clear skies, he got to the river early and had already caught two fish when Stigs showed up. Rosie had been up early too, wrestling with Hank in the sunshine, and wasn't interested in joining Raymond this morning.

"Where's our girl?" Stigs asked, sitting down next to Raymond.

"Nice to see you too," Raymond joked. "She was feeling lazy today."

Stigs was staring at Raymond and there was something about his look that made Raymond feel nervous.

Stigs sighed. "Listen, Raymond. I went by the Department of Social Services in Commerce this week."

Raymond nearly fell off the log. "You did what?" he asked, jumping to his feet.

"Now don't panic, kid. I needed to know that you were all right. You haven't been honest with me and I know something's been up with your folks."

"I told you everything was fine!" Raymond said angrily. His heart was beating into his throat. He could feel his muscles tensing and his hands began to tremble. The urge to run, to flee, was overwhelming.

"I didn't tell them anything, Raymond. I just asked a few questions about your parents. About your history."

"And?" Raymond almost screamed.

"And they couldn't tell me much, by law."

Raymond shook his head. His lips and throat were dry and he tried to swallow the dryness away. "That's because it's none of your business," he said.

"Maybe not," answered Stigs. "I'm sorry, Raymond. I know you've been taking care of yourself."

"So what?" Raymond spat. "I've been taking care of myself my whole life!"

Stigs stood slowly from the log, his arms out in surrender.

Raymond took a step back. "You don't know anything about me," he said.

He looked at Stigs and all he could see were his parents, his teachers, the children's home guardians, the car driving away down the street. Why did Stigs have to go to Social Services? Why couldn't he just leave it alone?

Raymond bent to gather his things and fumbled with the fishing rod. Stigs reached out and gripped the sleeve of Raymond's shirt, trying to get him to face him. Raymond jerked away. He overcorrected and fell into the dirt, scrambling to get up.

"Come on, kid," Stigs said, throwing his hands up again. "I'm just trying to help."

But Raymond didn't want help. He didn't want anything at all from the old man. He just wanted to get away from this conversation, get away from what was happening right now. He grabbed his fishing pole and tackle box and scrambled up the bank to the road, leaving his two fish and Stigs back at the river. He ran down the stretch of highway until he was around the curve. Then he darted into the woods.

He ran until he made it back to the hollow, startling Rosie and Hank from a nap. He paced the length of the camp. How could he have been so careless? He thought of Stigs at the river. He had just left him standing there. Now the empty feeling in his stomach was for something worse than just hunger. He crawled into the mouth of the hollow and held his knees to his chest. Then he buried his face in the sleeping bag and screamed.

He didn't go back to the river the next day or that Monday when the school was closed, worried that Stigs would show up. Instead, he stayed up late and tried his luck at night fishing. He was actually pretty successful at it. He wished that he could go tell Stigs about his discovery but he dismissed the thought as quickly as he'd had it. After school, he stayed in the camp, set his trap, and scavenged the dumpsters. He read, whittled, did his homework, played with Rosie and Hank, and tried to stay busy. After all, he had Harlin and Lexi. He didn't really need Stigs. He almost convinced himself. Almost.

Chapter Twenty

"You feeling okay, Ray?" Harlin asked in art. Raymond had spent the entire night before whittling a matching plate, bowl, and cup, along with an extra set of cutlery. By morning, he had a full set of dinnerware and his hands were calloused and sore from the constant work. But it had kept his mind occupied and off Stigs. It also kept him awake.

"Yeah, I'm fine," he said. Their art teacher tasked them with making white papier-mâché hearts that would be used as decorations for the semi-formal dance. Raymond wiped his forehead and dipped the paper in the glue mixture while Harlin cursed under his breath. Harlin's hands were covered in glue and he had bits of paper stuck to his fingers.

"It's just you look . . . well, you look terrible," Harlin said. He accidentally knocked over the pile of construction papers and scrambled to pick them up and get back in his seat. Then he lowered his voice. "Your parents showed back up?"

Raymond shook his head and tried to smile like it didn't bother him. "I'm fine, really. Just a little tired." Since his argument with Stigs, he hadn't been sleeping well at all. He tossed and turned at night, having nightmares of the children's home and Stigs and even Harlin and Lexi sometimes. He had tried everything he could think of to help him sleep. He tried making tea from leaves and bark, but that had only upset his stomach. He even tried jogging laps around the camp to try to expend more energy. Hank loved that, running circles around him as he jogged. He hadn't slept this poorly since his early nights in the hollow, before the sleeping bag, and before Stigs.

Hank had been around more, which usually made Raymond feel protected and helped him sleep. But over the last few nights, Raymond had realized how much noise Hank made. He snored, he tossed and turned, and his paws scratched the outside of the tree. He even howled sometimes in his sleep. Not full coyote howling, but it made Raymond wonder about Hank's dreams.

Harlin was looking at Raymond quizzically so Raymond tried to shift Harlin's attention.

"Your heart looks a little lopsided," he said. Harlin's heart looked more like a football to Raymond.

"This ain't even art," Harlin said, trying to scrape the paper from his fingertips.

Raymond laughed. "I thought you were excited about the dance?"

"My gran's making me go. I ain't keen on going alone. You sure you don't wanna go?"

"I'm sure," Raymond said, smiling at the thought of Harlin all dressed up for a dance. He thought of Lexi and quickly pushed the thought from his mind. Even if he had something to wear, he couldn't go to a dance.

The science fair was held that Thursday in the school's library. All the science teachers in the building acted as judges, walking through the library with clipboards, making their decisions while their students followed after them, looking at the projects. After school, parents and staff were invited to come and participate in the award ceremony. Raymond and Lexi took home third place, losing to the first-place project called "Solar-Powered Living." They stood on a little stage with the other winners as Mr. Rosen presented the awards. To Raymond's extreme displeasure, Joseph took second place with a project on sports drinks and their ability to contribute to endurance.

"Good grief," Lexi whispered to Raymond. "How hard is it to drink a bunch of Gatorade and see how fast you can run?"

As much as Raymond disliked Joseph, he had to admit that his project was impressive. Joseph had recorded himself testing his hypothesis and had mounted a tablet to his display board. Raymond and Lexi watched as a tiny Joseph ran across the screen over and over.

"He's on the cross-country team and I've seen him run. Trust me, he needs all the help he can get," Lexi said. Raymond smiled. He hadn't realized how competitive Lexi was. Raymond could see Lexi's mother and father standing among the parents, along with Lexi's little sister. Raymond thought she looked like a miniature version of Lexi with red pigtails.

"Maybe we should've included Gatorade in our experiment," he said.

"I guess there's always next year." Lexi shrugged and Raymond's chest swelled at the prospect of another project with

Lexi. "Be right back," she said when the ceremony was done, and she made her way over to her family.

Raymond watched as Joseph's father hugged him, clapping him on the back, genuinely proud. A knot formed in Raymond's stomach. Joseph caught his eye and Raymond quickly stared down at his shoes. Joseph's mother and Lexi's mother were laughing about something and Raymond wished he could ask what was funny. Even though he was a science fair winner like every other kid in the library, he felt out of place. He looked around and realized that he was the only student there without a parent. He fumbled with the third-place ribbon and tried to become invisible, concentrating on the pattern the linoleum floor made instead, counting the little squares.

When he looked up again, Stigs was standing in the doorway of the library. Before Raymond could move, Ms. Marcus was standing in front of Stigs with her hands on her hips. She looked different. Worried? Sad? Maybe both. How did Ms. Marcus know Stigs? Finally, she turned her head toward Raymond, looking him right in the eye. It looked like she was going to cry. Then she softened, turned back to Stigs, shook her head, and walked through the doorway and out of sight.

Raymond was so shocked that he felt he couldn't have moved his feet from that spot even if he had wanted to. Stigs approached him slowly.

"How did you—" Raymond started.

"You didn't leave me any choice," Stigs said. His voice was practically a whisper but Raymond could hear the concern in it. "You didn't come back to the river, did you? I had to call the blasted school to see when this science thing was." Raymond looked back at the floor.

"I'm sorry, Raymond. I overstepped. I was just worried and—"

"I'm not going back to a children's home," Raymond said. It was almost a whisper but his voice was steady. "I am not—" he started again.

But Stigs cut him off before he could go on. "It's okay, kid. I understand. Trust me, I know how you feel. I mean, I wish you would tell me what's going on, but you don't have to. I took care of myself my whole life and look how well I turned out, eh?" Raymond could tell he was trying to be funny and he was grateful. "When you're ready, maybe?"

Raymond nodded. He looked around and then back at Stigs. Then he threw his arms around the old man and squeezed. Stigs was momentarily stunned but he clapped him on the back. "All right," he said, laughing. Raymond let go. He wished Harlin was there too.

"Well," Stigs said. "I guess I better get going."

"How do you know Ms. Marcus?" Raymond asked. He wasn't ready for Stigs to leave.

"Small town, remember?" Stigs said, and he forced a smile.

Raymond's brow creased.

Stigs cleared his throat. "I'll see you this weekend, then?" he asked.

Raymond nodded again. He felt like he should say something else, but he didn't know what. Stigs looked out of place in the school, and you could tell he felt it too.

"Nice ribbon," he said, then he pushed through the door. Raymond smiled and gripped the third-place ribbon. When he turned around, Joseph was standing there.

"Who was that?" Joseph asked.

"A friend," said Raymond.

"That old man is your friend?" Joseph said with obvious skepticism. "And he just shows up at a middle school science fair? Where are your parents, then?"

"None of your business," Raymond said, feeling a surge of confidence in the wake of Stigs's visit.

Raymond didn't know why Joseph was suddenly so interested in him. He wanted to get away from this conversation as quickly as possible. Joseph jabbed a finger in Raymond's chest. "You obviously have Lexi fooled but you haven't fooled me. Remember that."

Raymond took a step back, moving away from Joseph's finger. "Bye, Joseph," he said with finality, and walked past him. Lexi was waiting to introduce Raymond to her family. He should've been overjoyed to have Lexi's father shake his hand, but Joseph was still staring at him, which made it hard for Raymond to feel anything but uncomfortable.

The next day, Raymond was careful to stay away from Joseph. And Joseph, in turn, seemed to forget about their run-in. He seemed too preoccupied with talk of his science fair success and plans for the semi-formal. Raymond would catch him looking his way on occasion, but he never said anything else to him.

Chapter Twenty-One

That Saturday, when Raymond woke up and packed his fishing gear, Rosie wagged her tail and whined with excitement. Raymond laughed. "I know. I know," he said, patting her head. "I missed him too." Hank stood and stretched, and wagged his tail with Rosie. When Raymond and Rosie began to walk toward the river, Hank tried to come also.

"Oh," said Raymond, feeling a pang of guilt. "Sorry, Hank. You can't come, buddy." Hank's tail abruptly stopped wagging. "Come on. Don't be like that." Raymond patted his head. "You can come another time, huh?" Hank turned and jumped into the hollow. Raymond started to reprimand him but then thought better of it. Besides, what was a little coyote hair? He needed to clean out the hollow anyway.

Raymond gathered his minnows and dropped his gear off at their usual spot. Then, unable to sit and wait today, he walked through the woods to the road where Stigs usually parked and found him getting out of his car.

"Aren't you a sight for sore eyes!" Stigs called.

"Nice to see you too," Raymond said.

"I was talking to Rosie," said Stigs, and he bent to rub her ears. Raymond laughed and opened the trunk of Stigs's car.

"Have you ever been night fishing?" Raymond asked as they unloaded their gear at the river.

"Not in years," Stigs said. "Why? Have *you* been night fishing?"

Raymond smiled. "I caught over a dozen fish this week, just upriver a bit," he said. "I only kept about half of them but I couldn't stop. It was the best I'd ever done."

"Must be spawning," Stigs said. "You were lucky to catch them at the right time. Here." He tossed Raymond a bucket. Raymond reached to catch it and fell forward into the mud, smearing his face, which made both of them laugh. Rosie jumped around them in happiness.

At the river, the pair fished all morning. Raymond built a fire and they roasted the fish they caught over the flames. Raymond wanted to tell Stigs about Harlin's dad but it felt like a betrayal somehow so he decided not to. Instead, he told Stigs about Lexi and about Joseph Banker bothering him all the time. Around noon, Stigs handed Raymond a can of soda from his cooler.

"Is this a girl that you're interested in?" asked Stigs.

"No," said Raymond, feeling a little uncomfortable. "It's not like that with Lexi and me. We're just friends." He and Lexi *were* just friends, after all. She was nice to him and Raymond couldn't say that about most of the students at River Mill. Then, without thinking, he added, "There's a semi-formal dance next weekend."

Stigs was about to take a sip from his own soda but stopped, leaving it suspended in midair. "Oh yeah? You going?"

Raymond instantly regretted saying anything. "Nah," he

said, and took a long swig from the can so he wouldn't have to keep talking. Raymond could feel his ears reddening.

"I remember those school dances," said Stigs.

"You can remember that long ago?"

"Watch it," Stigs said. His tone was serious but he was grinning. "They used to make us all go. It meant a night off for our guardians."

Raymond nodded, taking another sip of his drink and Stigs fell silent, remembering. Then he said, "I met my wife at a school dance when I was about your age."

"You met your wife when you were twelve?" Raymond asked, surprised. Stigs had never mentioned anything about a wife but Raymond knew she must've existed at some point. He tried to imagine a twelve-year-old Stigs asking a girl to dance and the thought made him laugh out loud.

Stigs didn't seem to notice. "She was the prettiest girl I'd ever seen."

"Did you ask her to dance?" Raymond asked.

"I did."

"Then what happened?"

Stigs laughed. "That, my boy, is none of your business." He took one last swig of his soda and then crushed the can with his hand. "Why don't you want to go to this dance, anyway?"

Raymond shrugged. "Nothing to wear," he answered honestly. Stigs looked at Raymond. Then he began packing up his gear. "Where are you going?" It was only lunchtime and they had plans to fish all day.

"Home. Get your stuff. You're coming too."

Raymond moaned a little about missing a good day's fishing. But he had already caught and cleaned two fish for later so he didn't argue. He and Rosie followed Stigs through the woods to the car and they drove to the cabin in silence.

Raymond unloaded the gear and carried it in for Stigs, setting it on the table. "Back here," Stigs said, leading Raymond down the hall to the bedroom. Stigs opened his closet and Raymond's mouth fell open. On one side were women's clothes; dresses, flowered shirts, and even a Sunday hat. On the other side were men's clothes but they were far too small (and nice) to belong to Stigs.

Stigs cleared his throat. "I, um . . . I haven't gotten around to . . ."

"It's okay," said Raymond, sparing his friend from speaking the end of that sentence. Stigs had clearly been keeping his wife's and son's clothes for some time now and Raymond didn't need an explanation about why. "What happened to her?" he asked quietly.

Stigs sighed. "Leukemia. Been about twenty years now. My son was just about your age when it happened." Raymond nodded and Stigs was quiet for a moment, running his finger along the cuff of a dress. "Anyway," he said, "he was skinny like his mama. They might be a bit big for you but I'm sure you can find something in here to wear to that dance."

Raymond nodded. He walked to the closet and thumbed through some of the shirts. He selected a blue button-down with small yellow stripes. He tried it on and it almost fit.

"You could roll up the sleeves," Stigs suggested.

Raymond turned to thank him but he was gone, leaving Raymond alone in the room.

Raymond found a pair of dress pants that fit him, even without a belt. The shoes were all two sizes too big but he didn't think it would matter if he wore his tennis shoes instead. He laid the clothes neatly across his arm and closed the closet door.

Stigs was poking the fire when Raymond came out of the bedroom. He glanced over his shoulder at Raymond. "Good. You found something."

"Thank you," Raymond said, and he meant it. "Do you think I could leave these here and come over next week to get them? The dance isn't until Friday night and I don't want to mess them up before then."

"Sure," Stigs said. "Just throw 'em on your bed."

Raymond went to the spare bedroom. Stigs had said *your* bed. He laid the clothes on the quilt and wished that he could find a reason to stay the night.

Before Raymond could say anything else, Stigs said, "Best be going now."

"Right," Raymond said. "Okay. Well, I'll see you next Friday. I'll come by after school."

Stigs grunted and continued poking the fire. Raymond thought Stigs would offer him a ride, but the man was preoccupied with his own thoughts, so Raymond collected his things and called for Rosie to follow.

The sun was setting by the time they made it back to camp.

Hank was no longer lounging in the hollow and was nowhere in sight. Raymond sloppily made a fire, trying to beat the dusk. He was roasting a fish when Hank arrived, snapping a twig right behind Raymond. He jumped and dropped the fish into the fire. Rosie hadn't growled in warning like she usually did. Hank tilted his head as Raymond yelled, pulling the charred fish from the flames.

"Do you have to sneak up on me like that? Here," Raymond said, throwing him the ash-covered fish. Hank settled himself happily on the ground, cradling the fish between his paws and eating. Raymond rolled his eyes. "I liked it better when you brought us dinner and not the other way around." Hank didn't appear to notice. Raymond roasted the other fish and he and Rosie shared it. Then he brushed his teeth and crawled into his sleeping bag.

He lay there trying to sleep, listening to Hank rustling around outside. He thought about the dance. Harlin would be happy that he was going, at least. He thought about the clothes in Stigs's closet and the people who used to wear them. He wondered how long the old man had been all alone in the cabin. *There are worse things than being alone*, Raymond reminded himself. He thought sleepily that Stigs really needed a dog . . . and maybe a coyote.

Chapter Twenty-Two

At breakfast on Monday morning, when Raymond told Harlin that he would be going to the dance, Harlin said, "Well, hot dog! Maybe it won't be as miserable as I thought. I can't wait to ask a girl to dance. We'll be dancing machines, you just wait and see!"

Raymond shook his head at the thought of actually dancing with anyone.

"You think I'm joking? I've been brushing up on my moves. Been watching some videos," he said with a wink.

Raymond wondered if Harlin was kidding but one look at his friend told him that he definitely was not. He hoped Harlin wouldn't make too big a fool of himself. And Raymond too, for that matter.

In science, Raymond sat down and said hello to Lexi, who was talking to a friend about dress shopping. Joseph tilted his head, smirking. "You going to the dance, Raymond?" He leaned back in his seat and propped his feet up on the table. "Not really your scene, is it?"

Raymond tried not to take the bait. He shrugged. "I might go," he said.

"Of course he is going," said Lexi. "Everyone is going. You are going, right, Raymond?"

Raymond nodded and tried not to blush but he thought his face would burst into flames.

"Good. See, Joseph? He's going. You can go back to minding your own business now."

Raymond had to look away to keep from smiling at the dumbstruck expression on Joseph's face.

Raymond felt himself growing more and more nervous as the week went on. The more folks talked about the dance, the more Raymond realized that he might actually have to dance with someone. His nerves nearly ate him alive. He went fishing, roasted his catch, did his homework, went to school, and found it increasingly hard to concentrate. He even considered throwing in the towel and just not going to the dance at all. But he thought of Lexi and changed his mind.

Harlin didn't seem bothered one bit by Raymond's lack of participation in their conversation during art each day. In fact, he seemed to be unusually quiet. Raymond began to worry that maybe Harlin was concerned about his father showing up.

"Everything good with you, Harlin?" Raymond asked.

Harlin took a few minutes to answer. He was obviously distracted by something. "What? Oh yeah. I'm good, buddy."

"Everything all right with your dad?" Raymond asked quietly.

A shadow fell across Harlin's face, and Raymond wished he

hadn't said anything. Harlin obviously hadn't been thinking about his dad until Raymond had gone and reminded him.

"My dad's fine. He's been spending some time at a place in Commerce. He's finally getting the help he needs. My gran says we can go see him once he's settled in. I guess I'll be taking my first trip out of River Mill."

"That's really good, Harlin," Raymond said. He still felt like he shouldn't have asked but he was happy to hear the news.

Harlin shook his head and then got quiet again, like he was concentrating. Raymond noticed that every so often Harlin's arms and feet would move or twitch, like he was dancing in his head. Harlin wasn't worried, he was *practicing*, Raymond thought, and he said a silent prayer that going to the dance wouldn't end like their attempt to go to the basketball game had.

Early Friday morning, Raymond woke up to a sunny sky with few clouds. It was going to be a warm day. That whole week, the temperature had been all over the place. It dipped down close to freezing one night and was sunny and warm the next day. Raymond had never lived in a state with such sporadic weather. He hadn't slept well the night before, feeling too nervous about the dance. Hank had left the camp the day before and Rosie was searching the woods for him.

It was one of the longest school days of Raymond's life.

They had another quiz in math that Raymond was sure he'd failed. His other classes seemed to drag on in a way they never did before. Finally, he made it to art. Harlin couldn't stop talking about the dance but Raymond was too tired and hungry to listen. He had barely eaten breakfast and lunch wasn't much better. His stomach was in knots and he wished that he had never agreed to go to this dance.

"I'll be here right at six," said Harlin. "You want to meet in front of the gym before we go in?"

"Sure. I'll try to be on time," Raymond agreed. He knew he would have to move fast to get to Stigs's and back before the dance started.

After school, he swung his book bag into the hollow and fed Rosie his uneaten breakfast. There was still no sign of Hank. He tried to get Rosie to stay but she wouldn't hear it, following him through the woods to Stigs's. Raymond ran most of the way and Rosie jogged along beside him. He finally made it up the long drive and into the cabin. Stigs was waiting in the bathroom with hair trimmers. Raymond's eyes widened.

"It's long overdue," Stigs said, gesturing for him to sit down on the toilet.

Raymond didn't argue, even when Stigs got out the electric razor. When he was finished, Raymond stood and looked in the mirror.

"Not bad," Stigs said. "Didn't even know you had a forehead under there, did ya?" He had shaved around the sides with the razor, leaving the top a little longer but not by much.

Raymond hardly recognized himself. "Thanks," he said.

"Why don't you take a shower to get the extra hair off?" Stigs suggested.

Raymond took a shower and scrubbed himself clean. He wished he could stay in the hot water for longer but he didn't want to be late for the dance. He got dressed in the spare room and checked the mirror in the bathroom one more time before leaving. He rubbed on some of Stigs's deodorant.

When he walked back into the living room, Stigs stood up. His smile was bigger than ever. "I feel like I should take a picture." Before Raymond could protest, Stigs laughed. "Only joking. You clean up real nice, kid."

"Thanks," Raymond said, feeling a little sheepish. "I'd better get going."

"What about Rosie?" Stigs asked. "You can't take her to the dance, can you?" Raymond hadn't thought about that. He couldn't explain that he could drop her off at camp before he went to the dance. Stigs eyed Raymond and then sighed. "Leave her with me. I'll bring her to the river tomorrow."

Rosie seemed overjoyed at the prospect. She barked and jumped up on the couch, lying down for the night. Raymond rolled his eyes.

"Okay," he said. "But just this once. Thank you," he added.

"Go, go," Stigs said, shooing him out the door.

Raymond walked as fast as he could back through the woods without actually running. He didn't own a watch. He usually went by the sun to tell time and he knew that he would be late meeting Harlin. Sure enough, when he made it to the front of the gym, Harlin was nowhere in sight. He could hear the sounds of music and laughter through the doors. He would have to brave the entrance alone. He took a deep breath and walked in.

The place was almost unrecognizable. The papier-mâché hearts they'd made in art class hung from the rafters. There were white twinkling lights strung along the walls and ceiling. There was a DJ in the corner and a table set up with drinks and snacks. A few kids were dancing, but most were standing around in clusters against the walls, huddled together and giggling.

Raymond didn't see Harlin anywhere and for one horrified minute, he thought maybe his friend hadn't come. But then he saw him. Harlin was in the middle of the dance floor, dancing to a fast-paced song with a girl Raymond had never seen before. He couldn't help but smile. Harlin wasn't kidding about his moves. He was keeping beat and everything. As soon as the song stopped, another began and Harlin went right back to dancing again, this time with another girl. After a slow song ended, Harlin made his way over to Raymond, who'd found a spot to sit in the bleachers.

"Hey, Ray! I was wondering if you was going to show up," he said. Harlin was dressed in his Sunday best, sporting a red bow tie and what looked like brand-new dancing shoes. He was sweating from exertion. "I hardly recognized you with your hair cut like that. It looks good." He wiped his brow with the back of his hand.

"Thanks," said Raymond, running a hand over his short hair.

"You seen Lexi?" Harlin asked.

Raymond's heart raced a little. "No, I haven't really looked," he lied. He had been scanning the gym for her red hair since the moment he walked through the door. He'd seen a few of Lexi's friends, but not her.

"She'll show," said Harlin. "Don't worry, buddy."

Raymond opened his mouth to say something but Harlin made a motion like he was zipping his lips.

Then Raymond saw her. She was making a beeline for a group of girls standing by the snack table. Raymond stood and was going to go talk to her, but then thought better of it. He sat back down and Harlin started talking about one of the girls he was dancing with. Raymond was barely listening. Lexi had braided her hair and wore a light pink dress that fell just above her knees. She looked around the gym, and when her eyes found Raymond, she smiled brightly and waved. He lifted a hand in response and she went back to talking to one of her friends. He exhaled.

Ten songs later and Raymond still hadn't moved a muscle, even to get a snack. His stomach growled. He couldn't bring himself to go talk to Lexi. Why did this feel so different from school? He talked to her all the time at school. And what about all those afternoons in the library? They were friends, weren't they? He was beginning to wonder why he'd come to this dance. He should have just stayed in his hollowed-out tree with his dog and his coyote.

Harlin continued to dance into the night, taking breaks every now and then to come and sit with Raymond.

"Ain't you going to dance?" he asked Raymond finally. He had removed the bow tie and his hair was wet with sweat. "The night is almost over, Ray. Go ask Lexi to dance."

Raymond shook his head.

"All right then, suit yourself." A girl on the dance floor called Harlin's name and Harlin headed back to the group he'd been dancing with all night.

Raymond watched Lexi and her friends dancing. The music was fast and Raymond wasn't about to try out his nonexistent dance moves and embarrass himself. He watched Lexi laugh as her friend twirled her around. Raymond sighed. Maybe he and Lexi weren't such good friends as he had thought. She hadn't come over to talk to him either, after all.

Then the DJ came over the mic system and announced that he was about to play the last two songs. Raymond felt his heart beat faster as Lexi chatted quietly on the dance floor with her friends, waiting for the song to start. Raymond took a deep breath and resolved to try. He stood up. He had taken two steps in Lexi's direction when he saw Joseph Banker ask her to dance. He couldn't see Lexi's response but when the music started, he could tell well enough what her answer had been. His heart sank as he watched Joseph put his arms around Lexi's waist.

That was it. He couldn't take it anymore. He turned and walked out of the gym, unbuttoning the top buttons of his shirt as he did. He sat down on the stoop by the parking lot and kicked pebbles. He would just go back to the hollow and pretend this night had never happened. He stood to leave.

"Raymond?" said a voice from behind him. It was Lexi. He turned to face her. "Are you leaving?" she asked.

"I . . . Well, yeah. I was."

"Oh," Lexi said, looking at her hands.

"You look really pretty," Raymond said quickly. "I like your dress."

Lexi looked up at him. "Thanks. I like your haircut."

Raymond's whole body felt warm. "Thanks."

It was quiet for what seemed like the longest few seconds of Raymond's life. He couldn't think of anything to say.

"Well, I better get back inside," she finally said. "I'll see you on Monday, Raymond."

"See you Monday." He watched her walk back into the gym.

Raymond drifted to the hollow in a daze. Hank was curled up at the base of the tree when Raymond made it home. He patted the coyote's head and pulled himself into the hollow. He lay on top of the sleeping bag with his arms crossed behind his head. Looking out into the night, he fell asleep. It was the first time in years that Raymond had forgotten to brush his teeth.

Raymond woke up early the next morning, got dressed, and folded up the borrowed clothes to return. He wished he could wash them first but there wasn't enough time to let them dry before he met Stigs. It was still warm out and the sun wasn't even up yet. Hank ran a few circles around the camp before bounding after something into the woods and out of sight.

Raymond walked along the edge of the hollow to the soft dirt and leaves. He gathered worms, grubs, and little insects: anything that he could find. He dropped them in the bottom of the empty milk jug. When he was happy with his collection, he packed his gear and the borrowed clothes in his duffel and headed to Stigs's cabin. Raymond worried that Stigs would also be up early so he picked up the pace, wanting to surprise him.

When he got to the cabin, he shed his coat and hat, sweating from the long walk. A small plume of smoke was trailing from the chimney stack on top of the little house and Raymond smiled. He went around back to the chicken coop. He opened the gate and called, "Come on, girls!" At the sound of his voice, the hens came running. Raymond scattered his offering of worms and bugs, and the hens happily accepted, flapping and cackling. When they were finished, they raced for the door. Raymond laughed. He grabbed the basket that hung on the wall and gathered up the eggs. He raked out the mulch and refilled the water bowls from the spigot on the side of the house.

When he was almost finished, he heard Stigs come rushing out of the cabin. Rosie trotted along behind him.

"What in the—" he started but he grinned when he saw Raymond. "You nearly gave me a heart attack. I thought a coyote had broken into the pen."

"Not quite," said Raymond. "I just wanted to come by and

surprise you. You're always helping me so I thought I would return the favor."

Stigs gestured to the milk jug in Raymond's hand. "Go ahead and fill that up and take it with you. I have more than enough."

Raymond thanked him and filled the jug with eggs. "Should we go fishing?" he asked when he was finished.

Stigs nodded. Raymond tried to put the borrowed clothes back inside but Stigs wouldn't hear of it. "Keep 'em," he said. "They don't get any use hanging in the closet."

Raymond was grateful. He could use the extra clothes. He helped Stigs load his fishing gear in the car and then he piled his own in. Rosie jumped happily into the back seat and Stigs rolled the window down for her to stick her head out.

There was a long silence before Stigs looked at Raymond. "Well?" he asked. "How was it?"

"Good," Raymond replied. He told Stigs all about Harlin's dancing. Stigs got a kick out of that.

"I'd like to meet that boy one day," he said, and laughed.

"Yeah. He's something." Then Raymond told Stigs about Lexi. He told him how he wished he could've asked her to dance and about Joseph Banker beating him to it. He left out the part about Lexi following him outside.

"You'll get another chance," Stigs said when they made it to the river. "But you can't go waiting around for something to happen. Opportunities come and go and eventually, you don't get any more chances, so you have to take the ones you get."

Raymond nodded, hoping he would in fact get another chance.

Raymond walked back to camp that afternoon with a milk jug full of eggs and three fish. He tossed one to Hank as he unpacked his gear. He spent the evening roasting fish and playing fetch with Hank and Rosie. Then he tidied his camp, cleaned up in the river, brushed his teeth, crawled into the hollow, and fell right to sleep.

Chapter Twenty-Three

On Monday, Harlin sat down at breakfast grinning. He was back in his regular attire, NASCAR T-shirt and blue jeans. But he seemed different, more confident, definitely more cheerful than usual, and just as chatty.

". . . but that last song was a good one," he finished a long story about the dance and the DJ and took a sip of his milk. A group of girls walked past the table, and Harlin waved, smiling from ear to ear.

After they passed, he looked at Raymond. "Where'd you go anyway? After the dance?"

Raymond shook his head. "I just had to get out of there."

Harlin gave him a knowing look. "Yeah," he said, taking a bite of his doughnut and talking with his mouth full. "I saw Lexi dancing with Joseph. Sorry, man. But after the dance, when we were all waiting outside to get picked up, I saw him try to talk to her again and she just ignored him. Left him standing there by himself while she talked to her friends."

Raymond was about to tell his friend how happy those words had made him but before he had the chance, the same troupe of girls passed again, carrying breakfast trays now.

"Hey, Harlin," a girl called.

Harlin grinned and said, "Hello, Samantha. Ladies." He nodded, as cool as a movie star. Raymond sat staring at Harlin.

Harlin tried to feign indifference. Then he stuffed the rest of the doughnut in his mouth, smearing powdered sugar across his cheek. "What? Do I have something on my face?" Harlin asked, trying to rub off the sugar.

"Um. What just happened?" Raymond said, gesturing to the group of girls that had just passed.

"Oh that." Harlin shrugged and grinned his biggest grin of all. "I guess I made some new friends at the dance."

The girls giggled from two tables over. "I guess you did," Raymond said, smiling back at his friend.

After a few minutes, Harlin looked around to make sure nobody was listening and leaned forward. "My gran says we're going to see my dad this week and I'll miss a couple of days of school."

Harlin definitely seemed optimistic to Raymond. Raymond didn't have much faith in parents, but he hoped beyond hope that everything would turn out okay for Harlin and his dad.

"How far is Commerce anyway?" Raymond asked. He didn't think it could be that far because he'd heard other kids talk about going there all the time. Before Harlin could answer, Lexi sat down in the empty chair next to Raymond.

"Hi," she said, and took a bite of her doughnut.

"Hi," said Raymond, his spirits brightening.

"Can I eat breakfast here?" Lexi asked. Raymond had only seen Lexi eating breakfast in the cafeteria on a few occasions and she usually sat with her friends.

Raymond grinned. "Sure. Fine with us. Right, Harlin?" He looked at Harlin, who nodded, suddenly speechless.

"What were you guys talking about?" Lexi asked.

Harlin gave Raymond a look.

"Nothing," Raymond said. "Harlin was telling me about the recent change in the NASCAR lineup." Raymond wasn't sure if he was talking gibberish or not but it sounded good to him.

"The new driver for 36?" Lexi asked, and Harlin nearly spit his milk across the table. Lexi pretended not to notice. "He's a rookie out of Louisiana," she continued, "but his numbers are good. I think he'll definitely mix things up this season."

Raymond thought Harlin might fall out of his chair. "*You* know NASCAR?" Harlin gawked.

"I follow my favorite drivers. Who doesn't?" Lexi shrugged. Harlin looked over at Raymond, and Raymond couldn't help but laugh. Lexi and Harlin spent the rest of breakfast discussing the new rookie and the lineup for the professional teams. Raymond finished his breakfast in silence. Neither of his friends asked him for his thoughts on the subject and he didn't mind one bit.

Lexi was already in science when Raymond got to class. Before Raymond could say anything, Joseph Banker sat down and cut Raymond off.

"Hey, Lexi," he said in a voice that was way too sweet coming from him. "I had a good time at the dance on Friday."

Lexi smiled politely. Then she turned to Raymond. "Did

you start ratios in math today, Raymond?" Joseph snapped his mouth shut, eyeing Raymond.

Raymond was about to answer, but he was cut off again.

"What did you do, sleep in the dirt?" Joseph asked, in his usual snide tone.

Raymond ran his fingers through his hair. A piece of a leaf fell out and floated to the table. Raymond blushed, flicking it off the table. It must've been there all morning.

Lexi glared at Joseph but didn't say anything. Any confidence that Raymond had when he sat down had vanished. He sat quietly, trying not to make eye contact with Lexi. Mr. Rosen began his lecture on the circulatory system and handed out diagrams for them to follow along and take notes. Raymond worked quietly, trying to ignore the feeling that Lexi was watching him.

Finally, at the end of class, Lexi asked, "Do you want to meet after school this week? Maybe you could help me with this ratio stuff Mr. Brewer assigned. I feel like my eyes are crossing."

"Sure," he said. "I can meet any day."

Joseph was listening to every word from across the table.

"I can only do Wednesday this week. Because of cross-country. But you could come to my house after practice one day. If you want to, I mean."

Raymond didn't say anything. How would he get to Lexi's house? Raymond thought about what Stigs had said at the river about missing opportunities. But unless she lived within a five-mile radius of the school, he wasn't likely to be able to walk there and back and he certainly didn't have the money for bus fare. But he couldn't explain that to Lexi.

"Yeah, maybe," he said, and Lexi's face fell just a little.

"Okay," she said quietly. "We can always just meet in the library, if you want."

"What's the matter, Raymond? Your parents not have a car?" Joseph asked, interrupting.

Raymond didn't even look at him.

"The library is fine," Lexi whispered, and she smiled, trying to show Raymond that Joseph didn't matter. "Wednesday then?"

Raymond nodded. "I'll be there."

Raymond was quiet all through art. Joseph's words were still ringing in his ears. What *had* he been thinking? Did he think he would actually be able to have a normal friendship with Lexi? One where he went to her house and they hung out somewhere other than school? He couldn't exactly invite her over to his house. He couldn't even call her. Nothing about Raymond's life was normal.

Harlin could tell Raymond was in a bad mood and he tried to cheer him up. "Maybe you, Lexi, me, and Samantha could all go to a movie together sometime?" he asked. The suggestion only made Raymond more upset.

"No, Harlin. Just leave it alone, okay?" Raymond snapped.

At the end of class, Raymond left without saying goodbye.

Raymond's mood didn't improve the next day or the next. Mr. Brewer gave another pop quiz and Raymond was sure he failed it. Mr. Rosen assigned them group work in science and

Lexi asked Raymond if he wanted to work together. Raymond shook his head and worked alone. Joseph piped up that he needed a partner and Lexi grudgingly agreed. Raymond tried to block out their conversation but Joseph kept bringing up their dance. Raymond finally closed his book and moved to another table.

Raymond considered not even going to the library on Wednesday afternoon but when the time came, he did go, sitting down quietly across from Lexi. He heard a laugh from behind him and he turned to see Joseph sitting at a nearby table with one of his friends. They were glaring at Raymond. Raymond rolled his eyes and turned back to Lexi.

"Did I do something, Raymond?" She looked hurt as she searched his face.

Raymond's mood shifted immediately. He'd never wanted to do anything to make Lexi feel bad and he suddenly felt ashamed of his behavior that week.

"No," he said, and sighed. "I'm sorry. I guess I'm just preoccupied."

She nodded, looking at Joseph. She twiddled her pencil. "He's a jerk," she said. "Just ignore him. He's been that way since kindergarten." Raymond tried to smile but it was unconvincing.

"You know, we don't have to do this today," she said, looking at her math book. "I already bombed the quiz anyway. We could do something else."

"Like what?" Raymond asked.

She thought for a minute, then said, "Ms. Amber got a new

projector last week. We could watch a movie or something." Raymond raised an eyebrow. Ms. Amber was nowhere in sight. He hadn't known Lexi to be a rule-breaker and he was pretty sure that watching a movie in the library was against the rules. "Come on." She closed her book and stood up. "I'll show you."

Raymond followed Lexi to a little room in the back of the nonfiction section.

"I helped her set it up last week. She won't mind." She flipped on the lights. The room looked like it was being used more for storage than anything else. Books were stacked high and there were papers scattered on the floor. The projector looked clean and new, out of place in the dingy room. Lexi found a stack of DVDs on a shelf. "There aren't many choices. I don't even know most of these."

Raymond walked over and looked at the options. There was only one title that he recognized and he pulled it from the shelf.

"*The Outsiders*?" Lexi asked.

Raymond shrugged. "I liked the book."

"Okay," she said cheerfully, taking the case. "*The Outsiders* it is!" She popped the DVD in and the projector screen lit up. She turned the overhead lights off and sat down on an old beanbag chair opposite the screen. She gestured for Raymond to sit too. He pulled a library chair with a loose back from the corner and sat down next to her.

In the light of the screen, Lexi's face had an eerie blue glow. "He kinda reminds me of you," she said.

"Which one?"

"The quiet one. Johnny."

Raymond kept his eyes on Lexi when he answered. "How about the red-haired girl, then? Cherry? She kinda looks like you." He smiled when Lexi rolled her eyes.

"Everybody thinks redheads look the same." They were about half an hour into the movie when the door opened and the lights switched on.

"What are you two doing back here?" It was Ms. Amber. Joseph was standing behind her, smirking.

"We were just watching a movie," Lexi said sweetly, shrugging. "I didn't think you'd mind."

Ms. Amber looked from Lexi to Raymond. She was a short woman with wavy blond hair. She wore black-rimmed glasses and high-heeled shoes every day.

"Well, I would at least like to be asked first, Lexi. You know better than that."

"I'm sorry, Ms. Amber," Raymond said. "It was my idea."

Joseph made a noise behind Ms. Amber. "Get back to work," she snapped at him.

"But—"

"You heard me," she said, shooing him out of the room. Then she looked back to Lexi and Raymond. "You two, also. The library is closing in fifteen minutes."

They did as they were told, going back to their table. Raymond smiled at Lexi. "She won't mind, huh?" Lexi gave him an innocent look. He laughed.

After a minute, Raymond said, "I'd better go." He didn't

want to have to make up another excuse for not getting picked up.

"Okay. Maybe when cross-country is over, we will have more time to study."

"How's that going anyway?" Raymond asked.

Lexi rolled her eyes. "We have a meet coming up and I'm about the slowest on the team," she said. "I just don't have that kind of stamina. I should've tried out for volleyball instead of running, but I'm not that coordinated either."

"That's not true," Raymond said. "I've seen you dance, remember?"

"I haven't seen you dance, though," she said quietly.

"I was going to ask you—" Raymond started. Lexi was determinedly looking at the book in front of her. "But Joseph got there first."

She looked up. "That's okay," she said, and shrugged. "There will be other dances." Raymond thought that if he ever had another chance to ask Lexi to dance, boy, he would take it.

Chapter Twenty-Four

The next day, Raymond walked Lexi to the gymnasium for cross-country practice after school. "Our first meet is next week," she told Raymond. "Mount Olive Middle is coming in from Commerce. River Mill is hosting for the first time ever."

"That's good, isn't it?" he asked.

Lexi looked nervous. "I guess. I've improved my time, but I'm still one of the slowest on the team. I hate the thought of coming in last."

"You won't be last," said Raymond.

"Will you come? It's on Monday."

Raymond thought about his last attempt to join an athletic event but figured since Joseph was running too, he couldn't get into that much trouble. "Sure, I will," he said. "I'll be the one at the finish line cheering you on."

"You might be waiting for a while," she joked. "Bring Harlin. Then you won't have to wait alone."

"I'll ask him, but I'm not sure he will be able to. He's been pretty busy lately." Harlin was visiting his father in Commerce and didn't want the kids at school to know. Raymond would keep his secret.

Lexi smiled at Raymond and then checked her watch. "I have to go," she said. "I'm helping Coach mark the trails for the meet so we can practice running it before next week."

"Where do the trails go?" Raymond asked, suddenly aware that the hollow, while at least half a mile from the school, might not be far enough to keep the cross-country team from running by. The thought of Lexi finding his camp in the woods made Raymond feel sick.

"Mostly just right around the school. We can't go too deep into the woods in case someone gets hurt."

Raymond relaxed a little but still made a mental note to make sure he checked those markers. "Have fun," he said. He watched her jog into the gym, her hair shining in the sunlight.

Raymond grinned all the way to the hollow. He did that a lot lately. Stigs said his mouth would get permanently stuck like that if he kept it up, but Raymond couldn't help it. For the first time since that year he had spent at the coast with his parents, he felt truly happy. He was so happy, in fact, that he didn't even notice that he was being followed.

"Hey, guys!" Raymond said cheerfully when he reached his camp. Hank and Rosie were rolling around in the leaves, play fighting. Rosie jumped up at the intrusion and Hank nipped at her ankle. Raymond laughed. "Glad to see you two having fun." Rosie licked his outstretched hand. She sniffed his pockets for any trace of food. He pulled out a biscuit and gave it to her.

A twig snapped behind him and Hank jumped up. Raymond

whirled around and there was Joseph Banker, standing in the woods behind a tree. He stepped out into the sunlight.

"What are you doing out here, Joseph?" Raymond asked. Every muscle in his body was on high alert and he could feel the blood rushing to his face, heating his neck along the way.

"What are *you* doing out here, Raymond?" Joseph retorted. His eyes darted around the camp. "Do you *live* out here?"

"No," Raymond said defensively, and stepped in front of the tree hollow, trying to block it from Joseph's view. His sleeping bag was hanging out of the opening and his clothes hung across the roots, drying from a recent wash. "Get out of here, Joseph. You don't know what you're talking about." He took a step forward. Hank had also taken a few steps forward and was now standing directly behind Raymond.

"Is that a coyote?" Joseph asked, fear spreading across his face. He stumbled backward. "What's he doing?"

Hank's head was low and his eyes were locked on Joseph, his shoulder blades heightened.

"Tell it to stop." Joseph looked around, frantic. He grabbed a stick and swung it in front of him.

"Stop it, Joseph," Raymond hissed. "He won't hurt you." Raymond wasn't sure if he was right about that or not. In response, Hank growled and snapped his teeth at Joseph, who screamed and fell backward into the leaves.

"No, Hank!" Raymond yelled, and the coyote's forward march halted.

Joseph scrambled back, kicking up leaves. "It has a *name*? Who *are* you?" he screamed at Raymond, finding his footing.

He stood and shouted at Hank, swinging the stick. "Stay away from me!" Hank hadn't moved again since Raymond's command, and Joseph's eyes darted from Hank to Raymond.

Raymond's heart was racing and every impulse he had told him to keep Joseph talking. But Joseph was too panicked to listen.

"Stay away from me!" Joseph screamed. "Stay away from me or else."

Raymond couldn't tell if Joseph was talking to him or to Hank, but he didn't have time to ask. Joseph threw the stick at them and raced away, back in the direction of the school, leaving Raymond to watch him go.

Hank turned to Raymond and stretched his jaw, yawning.

"Stay here," Raymond whispered to the coyote. But Raymond couldn't stay there. Not now. Joseph would be back at the school any minute and then what? He would tell everyone that Raymond was living in the woods with a wild coyote.

"We have to go," he told Rosie and Hank, and his muscles jerked into action. He ran to the hollow and pulled the clothes off the roots. He stuffed them into his duffel. He grabbed his fishing gear, his books, and his little wooden statues and stuffed them in too. He quickly rolled the sleeping bag, haphazardly tying it into a bundle. He looked around for any other evidence that someone lived there. He kicked the lean-to over, smashing the roof and scattering the sticks below it. He sloppily kicked leaves and brush over his firepit and tried to scatter them around the camp.

He looked around quickly to make sure he hadn't left

anything. His eyes lingered on the tree that had been his home for the past two months. Then he beckoned for Rosie and Hank to follow as he ran into the woods. He needed to get as far away from the school as possible. When he got to the river, he listened for any signs that someone was following. He strained to hear anything—voices, footsteps, anything at all—but it was silent. He kept moving along the river until he reached a spot that he had never been to before.

"Get out of here, Hank," he whispered, but the animal didn't move. "Go, Hank. They'll be looking for you." Hank sat down in the sand and scratched his ear with his back paw. Raymond picked up a rock and threw it. It thumped a few feet from Hank and he ignored it. "Go!" Raymond half shouted, still trying to keep his voice down. Hank looked at Raymond for a few seconds and then he turned and trotted into the woods. Raymond stowed his belongings behind a small rock formation by the water and tried to conceal himself in the brush. How long did he stay there, crouched like a hunted animal in the bushes? Minutes? Hours? He lost track of time, waiting. Waiting for what? Someone to come and drag him out. And take him where? Raymond balled his hands into fists and beat the earth beneath him. How could he have been so careless? How could he not have known someone was following him?

He went over and over the encounter with Joseph in his head until he couldn't think about it anymore. And then he thought of Lexi. What would she think? What would she say? Raymond sank his head into his hands and rocked back and forth in the sandy earth. Hot tears poured down his cheeks and Rosie tried to lick them away.

Raymond stayed there, crouched in the bushes until the sun set and the air turned chilly. It began to rain, and Raymond pulled himself deeper into the brush, not wanting to risk coming out into the open to get his things from behind the rocks. He waited there into the night but nobody came. Nobody called his name. No search party. No police sirens. Nothing.

In the early hours of the next day, Raymond emerged from the brush and paced back and forth beside the river. He tried to think of what to do. He didn't think he could go to school. He pictured Joseph waiting to out Raymond in front of a crowd. He could go to Stigs, but he knew Stigs wouldn't be okay with harboring an abandoned kid. He could run. But where would he go? He didn't have any family and he had never stayed in a place long enough to make friends. Except for River Mill. He thought of Lexi and Harlin and wondered if they would help him if he asked. Even if one of them was willing, what could they really do? Raymond ran through every available option and couldn't come up with a solution. This had been his solution, after all. Living in the woods.

He would have to leave River Mill. He wasn't willing to risk getting forced into a children's home again. He had long since given up cursing his parents for all of this but he couldn't help but think of them now. How many nights had he spent wondering where they were and if they would come back? But they weren't coming back. Raymond was done wishing for things that would never happen. He would just have to start over somewhere else. On his own. He didn't want to leave without saying goodbye to Lexi and Harlin, but he couldn't risk doing that until after school. He sat on the bank of the river for a long time. The sun was shining and Raymond could feel the heat on his scalp. He got up and unrolled the sleeping bag, laying it in the sun to dry. He left his clothes in the duffel. He didn't want to have to pack up again if he needed to make a quick getaway.

His stomach growled. The last time Raymond had eaten had been at lunch the day before. That felt like a lifetime ago. The river was different in this stretch of the woods. It was rockier and the brush was denser here. He thought he might have okay luck catching a fish in the tall weeds that ran along the side of the bank.

He cast his line from the shore. It got hung up on a tree branch and he yanked it, trying to pull it free. The line snapped and Raymond lost his footing, stepping into the marshy water. Something sharp struck his calf.

The snake wasn't hard to spot as it released Raymond's leg and darted back into the river grass. It was a cottonmouth, long and lean, dark and glistening from the sun. It recoiled and dove under the water. Raymond watched it just long enough to see the tail disappear before he leaped from the water to the shore, falling to his hands and knees.

He inspected the bite. It was red and something was oozing from two small punctures. His calf was already swollen, making it hard to pull up his jeans. An unnatural heat was working its way up Raymond's leg. He felt dizzy and he tried to stand but retched into the sand instead, falling back down. Rosie was whining beside him, panting. She licked his face. "It's okay, girl," he tried to say, but he coughed and heaved again, spitting up stomach bile. He tried to crawl to his duffel bag but his head was pounding and his vision was blurry. Rosie was barking and he wished she would stop. He fell to the ground and the world went dark.

Chapter Twenty-Five

When Raymond woke up, it was to the sounds of a machine beeping. He opened his eyes slowly, letting them adjust to the glare of the fluorescent lights. His head was reeling. A woman with dark curls was standing over him.

"Where am I?" Raymond tried to ask. His voice was cracked and dry. He desperately wanted a glass of water.

"Shh," the woman said. "You're at the hospital. You were bitten by a snake."

The memory of the snakebite came flooding back to him and with it, the memory of Joseph Banker finding him in the woods. He tried to sit up but instantly realized his mistake, bending over to vomit into the waste bin beside his head.

"Easy now," the woman cooed, adjusting something by Raymond's arm. And his eyes closed again.

When he woke up for a second time, it was Ms. Marcus's voice that finally stirred him. This time he kept his eyes closed. "Raymond? You okay, sweetie? We've been so worried."

"Worried?" Harlin's voice broke in. "He's been living in the woods! He's all anyone is talking about."

"Hush, Harlin," Ms. Marcus said. "I told the nurse you wouldn't get him riled up."

Raymond peered at them.

Harlin grinned and yelled, "Well hey there, bud—"

"Harlin!" Ms. Marcus interrupted.

"Sorry," he said, lowering his voice. "Hey there, Ray," he said in a whisper.

Raymond tried to grin. Harlin was a sight for sore eyes. Literally. Every muscle in Raymond's body was sore and achy.

"What happened?" Raymond croaked.

Ms. Marcus rested her hand on Raymond's shoulder. "Raymond, you were bitten by a snake. But you're going to be fine. The doctors have given you antivenom and said you'd be sore for a few days. Stigs found you by the river. He's on his way back to the hospital now. He had to take your dog home. They wouldn't let him bring her in."

Raymond tried to nod but his head was throbbing and he closed his eyes tight.

"Just rest now," Ms. Marcus said. "We'll sort everything out later."

Raymond had more questions, but every time he tried to talk, he felt sick to his stomach again so he laid his head back on the pillow and kept his eyes closed.

The next time he opened them, Stigs was in an armchair by the window, sleeping. Raymond could hear Harlin arguing in the hall with a woman who Raymond could only assume was his gran.

"He's my buddy," Harlin was saying. "I'm staying." His gran muttered something but Raymond couldn't hear all that well.

Raymond felt a little steadier than he did before. The door clicked closed behind Harlin, and Stigs opened his eyes.

"Hey," Raymond said.

"How are you feeling, kid?" Stigs asked, wiping the sleep from his eyes.

"I'm okay," Raymond lied. His head was still pounding and his leg was aching. But he didn't feel as dizzy as he had before and his fever had mostly lifted. "How did you—" Raymond started.

"You have a heckuva dog," Stigs said. "I was chopping wood when Rosie came running up my driveway barking and going crazy. I thought she was going to pass out, she was so keyed up. I followed her and she led me to you. The police got there about the same time that I did."

"The police?"

"Yeah," Harlin cut in. "Joseph told Mrs. Harding what happened the other day in the woods. The whole school knows by now. Sorry, buddy."

Raymond groaned, thinking of Lexi. He had really wanted to explain everything to her himself. Now he wouldn't have the chance.

Harlin continued: "Mrs. Harding called the police after you didn't show up for school. They drove in, lights blazing, and started searching the woods out back. I guess they found you at the river. You'd think you were a wanted fugitive or something instead of just a missing kid."

Raymond felt sick to his stomach.

"It took us a while to get to you," Stigs said. "A coyote was standing over you when we got there. I thought you must've been attacked. The police did too. We didn't even realize that you had a snakebite until we got you to the ambulance and you started moaning about a cottonmouth. Then we saw your leg all swollen up like it was."

Raymond stared at Stigs. He swallowed. "What happened to the coyote?" Raymond asked. Nobody answered. "What happened?" he asked again, his eyes pleading.

"The police . . . well, they shot him, Raymond."

Raymond closed his eyes and tried not to hear it. He tried to make it not true. It couldn't be true. Hank wasn't dead. Sweet, playful, rabbit-catching Hank. Tears poured down his face.

"They thought he was attacking you, Raymond," Stigs said quietly. "I did too. We didn't realize . . ." But he didn't finish the sentence.

They didn't realize, Raymond thought, that he had been living in the woods with a wild coyote. They didn't realize that a coyote could be protective instead of rabid, like Joseph had surely told them he was.

"Hank," Raymond said finally, choking out the name. "His name was Hank."

"I'm sorry, Ray," Harlin said. "But what were you doing living in the woods all this time? And with a coyote too? You said your parents weren't around but I never thought . . . That was why you needed the sleeping bag so bad, huh?"

It was Raymond's turn to apologize. He knew that. He had been lying to everyone for so long. He looked at Harlin and then at Stigs.

"I'm sorry," he said, shaking his head. He wiped his face with his sleeve. "I'm sorry." He had to catch his breath to keep from coughing through the tears. The nurse walked in and told Stigs and Harlin that Raymond needed his rest and if they couldn't keep it down, they would have to leave. Raymond took a few deep breaths and steadied himself. He tried not to think of Hank.

The nurse checked Raymond's machines, got him a pitcher of water, and left the room. He poured a cup and drank the whole thing.

"What's going to happen now?" he asked when he was finished, looking at Stigs. "I can't go back to the children's home. It's all white walls and fake air. No trees. No river. No fishing. Please," he begged. "Please don't make me go back." He was crying again and Harlin wiped his eyes too, quiet at the foot of Raymond's bed.

"I don't know, Raymond," Stigs answered. "They are trying to locate your folks. But there doesn't seem to be any sign of them anywhere."

Raymond looked at the ceiling. "They won't find them," he said. He knew they wouldn't. They were gone for good and Raymond couldn't decide if that made him feel better or worse.

"Natalie is real upset about all this," Stigs said. "Said she saw you go into the woods one day. She's out there talking to the social workers now. I imagine they'll want to talk to you soon too."

"Natalie?" Raymond asked, and then he realized Stigs was talking about Ms. Marcus. He hadn't known her first name. "How does she know you?"

Stigs looked at the floor and sighed. "I was going to be her father-in-law not too long ago. But, well, things went the way they went."

Raymond understood now. Ms. Marcus had been going to marry Stigs's son. No wonder she looked so sad when she saw Stigs's name on Raymond's paper that day.

"We should've been family. I didn't do right by her. I should've been there." Stigs swallowed. "But I was too messed up on my own to take care of anyone else. She did everything. The funeral, the arrangements, everything." Stigs looked up now and Raymond could see that he was crying. "I blamed myself for what happened but you can't go around blaming yourself for other people's decisions. I shouldn't have then and you can't now. None of this is your fault, son. None of it."

Just then, Ms. Marcus opened the door and stuck her head in. "Harlin," she said. "Your gran says she can't wait any longer." She stepped into the room.

"All right then," Harlin said. He looked at Raymond. "I'll come back as soon as I can. Want me to tell anyone anything?"

Raymond knew he was talking about Lexi, but what could he possibly say that would make any of this better? Raymond shook his head, and Harlin left the room.

Ms. Marcus looked at Stigs. "They would like to speak to you now," she said. Stigs looked at Raymond for a long time before getting up.

When the door closed behind him, Ms. Marcus tried to smile at Raymond. "How are you feeling?" she asked.

"A little woozy."

"Raymond, I—" But she stopped as suddenly as she had started.

"Am I going to have to go into a children's home now?" he asked, trying to keep his voice steady.

She sighed. "I'm not sure, Raymond. There aren't many foster homes around here. That'll be up to the state, I suppose."

Raymond laid his head back on the pillow to stare at the ceiling. "What about Rosie?" His eyes were locked on a flaking spot of paint above his head. "Can I see my dog?"

"I'm sorry," she said. "Stigs took her to the cabin. They won't let her in the hospital."

Raymond pinched his eyes shut to the tears that were flowing again.

Ms. Marcus put her hand on his shoulder. "You rest now," she said, and left him alone in the room.

Stigs didn't come back for a long time after that, and when he did, his eyes looked swollen. He walked to the edge of the hospital bed. "Listen, Raymond," he said. "I told them you could come and stay with me. I want you to know that. I tried, Raymond. But they . . . well, they don't agree. They're probably right." He sighed.

Raymond felt numb. He swallowed, trying to hold back the tears that would only make Stigs feel worse. "Where are they sending me?" he asked.

"There's a couple in Commerce that's agreed to take you in. They've been in the foster program for a while now but they haven't had anyone stay with them for a few years. They'll be coming in tomorrow to meet you."

Raymond nodded. This was what he had been trying so hard to avoid. And after everything, he had failed. He would be going back into the system and there wasn't anything he could do about it. Foster care. What would that be like? Raymond hadn't heard of one good experience about foster care from the kids in the children's home and he imagined it would probably be the same or worse for him. He ran through his options and didn't come up with much. He had no money. They would know to look for him at Stigs's or Harlin's. He could sneak out of the hospital and head for the woods on his own but he didn't think he would get too far with his leg the way it was. And then there was Rosie. He couldn't leave Rosie.

"What about Rosie?" he asked. "Can she come too?"

Stigs shrugged. "I'm not sure," he said.

Raymond couldn't bear it without Rosie. He had cried more that day than he had ever cried before and well, he just couldn't do it anymore. He laid his head back on the pillow and tried not to think of foster care, or Rosie, or Hank.

The nurse came in to tell them that visiting hours were over unless you were family but Stigs didn't move. "I am family," he said. The nurse looked like she was going to argue but then changed her mind.

"Fine," she said quietly. She checked Raymond's IV and closed the door again behind her.

"It's all right," Raymond told Stigs. "You can go. Rosie will be waiting for you. I don't want her to be alone."

"And what about you?" Stigs asked.

"I'll be fine." Raymond tried to smile. "Really."

Stigs stayed through dinner anyway but Raymond couldn't stomach much. He ate a few crackers and resisted the urge to pocket the rest of his dinner for Rosie. He didn't need to do that anymore.

Before Stigs left, Raymond asked, "Will you bury him for me? Hank? He deserves that much."

Stigs promised to do it first thing in the morning. "Try and get some sleep," he said, and pulled the door shut behind him.

Raymond lay in the hospital bed into the evening, staring at the ceiling. He thought of Rosie. And Hank. He thought of Harlin and Lexi. Of Ms. Marcus and Stigs. He thought of his parents and he felt so sad that he thought he might break in two.

At two in the morning, the door to Raymond's room squeaked open. "Raymond?" a voice whispered. It was Lexi.

"Lexi," Raymond said, sitting up in bed. He had been drifting in and out of sleep but felt wide awake now. "How did you—"

"I took the bus," she said. "My parents think I'm sleeping. They'll be mad as fire if they wake up and find out I left. I wrote them a note just in case." Raymond stared at her, unsure of what to say. She walked to the side of the bed. "What happened, Raymond? Joseph said you attacked him. Have you really been living in the woods all this time?"

How could he explain himself? How could he tell her about his parents leaving and not giving him any other choice? He swallowed hard and started at the beginning.

When he was finished, Lexi stared at him. Somewhere in the middle of the story, she had started crying.

"I'm so sorry," Raymond said. "I wanted to tell you. I really did. But I . . . couldn't."

Lexi nodded. She found Raymond's hand and squeezed it. Her touch was warm, and Raymond could feel it all the way into his throat.

"They say I'm going to live with a couple in Commerce," he said finally. Lexi let go of his hand and Raymond immediately wished he hadn't said anything.

"Commerce," she repeated. She looked at him and tried to smile. "That's just one town over. We can still see each other all the time."

Raymond smiled at her. "It was you, wasn't it? It was you who put the toothpaste in my cubby and the five dollars in my math book. I thought it was Ms. Marcus, but it was you." Lexi smiled at him and shrugged.

"Sometimes I help Ms. Marcus check the notebooks and I read yours. I saw where you erased that you wanted toothpaste and, well, we have plenty of toothpaste lying around with my dad being a dentist."

"How did you know I needed the money?" he asked.

"I overheard you in the cafeteria that day. Your table was right next to ours. You told Harlin that you needed it to go to the Jamboree. And I guess I just . . . wanted you to go."

Raymond wondered how he ever could've missed Lexi sitting so close to him in the cafeteria. Even in the dim lights of the hospital, Raymond could see her blushing.

He found her hand again and pulled her down to meet him. He paused to make sure it was okay, and when she smiled, he kissed her. It was exactly as Raymond imagined it would be. He could smell the sweetness of her hair, like strawberries and springtime.

She stood and grinned at him. "I'll come again," she told him, and he reluctantly let her hand go.

Chapter Twenty-Six

The next day, Mr. and Mrs. Adams came from Commerce to meet Raymond. Their first names were Alice and Thomas. They seemed nice, not at all like the guardians at the children's home. They looked young except that Mr. Adams had a gray streak running through his hair. They told Raymond that they'd never had any children of their own, despite trying for years. But they had fostered two kids before who had become as good as theirs. They showed Raymond a family photo album full of pictures of holidays, vacations, graduations, and birthday parties.

"We told them about you," said Mr. Adams, "and they can't wait to meet you. Said they would drive in this weekend if you're ready."

Raymond nodded, looking at the photos.

"Mary is in college now but James lives just five minutes away from us, with his family," Mrs. Adams said, pointing to the two small twin boys in one of the pictures. "That's Henry and that's Charlie. I still say we are too young to be grandparents but look at us now."

Raymond looked at the pictures of the smiling faces and tried to imagine himself in the photos. It was hard to do. Everyone looked so happy. Raymond had never known a family to look like that. There were no photo albums at the children's home. His parents didn't have any photo albums either. It was hard to imagine being anywhere but on his own with Rosie.

"I'm excited to meet your dog," Mr. Adams said, and he looked genuinely enthusiastic. "It's been a long time since we've had any four-legged friends."

"Yeah," said Raymond quietly. "She likes Stigs better than me most of the time, so she'll probably love you." He gave a nervous smile but then he realized the Adams probably didn't know who Stigs was. "Sorry."

Mrs. Adams put her hand on his arm. "Don't apologize, sweetie. We know this is going to be hard. It'll be an adjustment for all of us."

"But we want you to know that we are so happy that you'll be coming to stay with us," Mr. Adams said. "We'll get it sorted out together."

Raymond noticed that when either of them spoke to him, they looked him right in the eye, something his parents had never done.

They told Raymond that they would be enrolling him in a middle school in Commerce but he could wait until he was healed and ready to return. Raymond hated the thought of another new school, but he nodded politely and tried to smile. When they left, they promised to be back the next day and Raymond was sorry to see them go.

That evening after everyone had gone home, Raymond lay awake in his bed, listening to the beeps and murmurs in the hospital wing outside his room. This was the longest he had been stuck inside since living in the children's home. He closed his eyes, took a deep breath, and exhaled slowly.

Raymond remembered watching a sitcom on television when he was little. It was about a family with a bunch of kids. They ate their meals at the table and they argued about the silliest things, like who was supposed to take the trash out or who got to use the telephone at night.

Raymond wondered if living with the Adamses would be like that. Except without the other kids. He wondered if they would eat their meals together at a table. He wondered if he would be able to go to the woods sometimes if he wanted to. Mostly, he wondered how he would fit into the Adamses' lives. This was the most nervous Raymond had ever been. He took another deep breath and closed his eyes. He could live in the woods in the middle of winter. He could feed himself, keep himself warm, take care of Rosie. But this? This was downright scary. And even though Raymond was scared of what his future would hold, he couldn't help but feel a little hopeful too.

Lexi and Harlin came to see Raymond every day that he was in the hospital. Sometimes they came on their own but mostly they came together.

Harlin filled Raymond in on his plans for the spring talent show. Apparently, Harlin's dance moves had drawn enough attention from a group of eighth-grade girls that they had asked him to help with their talent show routine. Harlin had humbly obliged.

"I heard Joseph and a few other boys have decided to enter the show as well, now that cross-country is over," Lexi told Raymond. "I think they are dancing too."

Harlin's face fell, so Lexi quickly added, "Don't worry, Harlin. You saw them at the dance. They're nothing special."

Harlin sighed and then shook his shoulders out like he was shaking off a heavy coat. "Just means I'll have to step up my game is all," he said.

"Cross-country!" Raymond said suddenly. "I missed your meet! I feel awful, Lexi. How did you do?"

"I came in second to last," she said, shrugging. "Maybe next year I'll try out for volleyball. Or something else that doesn't involve running."

Next year. Raymond wouldn't be there next year. He would be at a different middle school, one that felt very far away from Lexi and Harlin. When the nurse came in to tell them visiting hours were over, Harlin said goodbye and moon-walked out the door. Raymond laughed and waved goodbye to his friends.

"It's only one town over," Lexi reminded him again before she left.

"I know," he said, but it felt like so much farther.

The next day, Stigs brought Raymond a copy of the local

newspaper. Raymond read the article over and over and practically had it memorized. Harlin thumbed through it later. The headline read: "Abandoned Boy Survives in Woods Behind Middle School." The picture below it was of the hollowed tree. It looked like someone had built a fire, Raymond guessed, to make a more appealing photo. The article talked about Raymond's parents, still unfound. And there was a quote from Joseph about Raymond always keeping to himself even though he had tried to be his friend.

Harlin rolled his eyes. "Yeah right, like Joseph ever tried to be your friend." It was obvious that Harlin was more than a little upset that nobody had interviewed him about Raymond. "I would've set them straight," he mumbled.

Mostly, the article was about the school's accountability. "How," the article asked, "did nobody notice Raymond's living situation for almost three months of the school year?" Raymond felt bad for Mrs. Harding, who was called out by name in the article. It wasn't her fault. Raymond wished that he could tell her that.

He cut out the picture from the newspaper and threw away the rest. He tucked it into his duffel bag for safekeeping.

Mr. and Mrs. Adams came every day to visit Raymond in the hospital and on Friday, they came to take him home. They promised Raymond that he could visit River Mill as much as he wanted. Mr. Adams explained that his business was opening up a new tractor-supply store in town, so he would be traveling back and forth a lot over the next year anyway. He told Raymond he could use the company on the car rides.

"He's not much of a loner," Mrs. Adams said as she helped Raymond to their car. "He'll probably drive you crazy."

Raymond gave a nervous laugh. Mr. Adams said, "She's kidding. Mostly. But I do want you to give me some pointers on fishing. Your friend Stigs says you are quite the fisherman."

Raymond had said goodbye to Stigs the day before. Stigs had snuck Rosie into the hospital and cursed at the nurse when she tried to make them leave. That was the hardest goodbye Raymond had made. His throat tightened as he thought about it.

"I'd like to see you try and take her from me," Stigs said to someone in the hall as he shuffled into Raymond's hospital room.

Rosie jumped on the bed and licked Raymond's face until it was covered in dog slobber. "Rosie!" he said, and laughed. "Good girl, Rosie."

"She's been a mess. Liked to worry me to death wanting to see you. I'll be glad for a little peace and quiet for a while," Stigs said. But his eyes were heavy and Raymond could see a sadness in them.

"Thank you," Raymond offered.

Stigs shuffled uncomfortably. "Nah. Thank you, kid. I only wish I could've done more for you."

"You did plenty," Raymond said, and then he looked the old man square in the eyes. "You saved us." Stigs smiled and

Raymond recognized the look Stigs was giving him. It was a mixture of sadness, grief, and like he was still holding out hope for something. Stigs opened his mouth to say something, but then he shut it again, changing his mind. When he finally did speak, it was about Hank.

"I buried your friend on a high bank near our regular spot," he said. "It's clear and sunny and overlooks the river. I think you'd like it."

Raymond knew one day he would be able to think of Hank and smile, but right now all he felt was sorrow.

Stigs said he'd talked with Mr. and Mrs. Adams about Raymond maybe coming down to go fishing every once in a while.

"That would be great," Raymond said.

"That way I can see this ol' girl too," Stigs said, rubbing Rosie's back.

"Will you tell Ms. Marcus I said goodbye?" Raymond asked. He hadn't been able to talk to her after the last time and he didn't know if he would ever see her again.

Something shifted on Stigs's face and he nodded. "She's coming by later for dinner so I expect I can tell her then."

When it was time for Stigs to go, he patted Rosie's head and gave Raymond a little wave, leaving without saying goodbye. Raymond knew he meant to, though.

And he knew he would see the old man again.

Now, Raymond paused before getting into the car. It felt good to be outside again. His leg was still stiff but it was getting better. He had been walking on it a little each day, with the help of his nurses and friends.

"Come on, girl," he called to Rosie, who jumped in the back seat.

Raymond took a deep breath and then got in and buckled up. The hospital was on the opposite side of town but when they drove over the bridge, heading to Commerce, Raymond could see the river from his window. He thought of his camp and the hollow, lying abandoned once again in the woods. He thought of Hank and a lump swelled in his throat. He wished he could have thanked the coyote.

"Goodbye, Hank," he whispered.

"I'm hungry," Mr. Adams said from the front seat.

Raymond swallowed hard and wiped a final tear from his face. Rosie licked his cheek.

"You're always hungry," Mrs. Adams said, and laughed. "I'll get dinner ready as soon as we get home." She glanced at Raymond in the back seat. "I hope you like spaghetti."

Raymond let out a little laugh. In that moment, he felt hope creep up inside him again. Maybe the Adamses would be people he could count on. Maybe everything was going to work out. For the first time in a very long time, Raymond didn't want to be invisible anymore. For the first time in a very long time, Raymond wanted to be seen.

Acknowledgments

To my father, Mark Colgrove, who read and reread these pages with me, offering honesty and wisdom and insight with every turn, thank you.

I want to thank my agent, Mary Cummings, for the first email she ever sent to me. It changed my life. Thank you for always wording things just exactly how I need to hear them in order to be successful.

Thanks also to Janine O'Malley, for your patience and vision on this project. You are a wonder and I feel so lucky to work with you.

Alex Rudd, your support, love, friendship, and overall enthusiasm for my work remain among my greatest blessings. Thank you.

To everyone who read my first and second and third drafts, thank you. In particular, my aunt Linda Crittenden, my nephew Benjamin Colgrove, my mother, Sharon Colgrove, and my sisters, Klesa Ausherman and Julia Blaine. You are the best team a girl could ever hope for.

Important note: This book and the characters in it are works of fiction. I want to acknowledge the students, staff, and administration at Southern Middle School for your encouraging words, acceptance, kindness, and overall support.

Special thanks also to Kim Adcock, Thomas Blaine, Adam Rudd, and Emily Kremer for answering all my questions.